I0537536

DEDICATED TO MY TEACHERS AND FAMILY,
SPECIFICALLY MY PARENTS, WHO DEDICATED SO
MUCH TO ME... THANK YOU

•••

PREFACE

WRITTEN AND CREATED BY A LOCAL CHICAGO ARTIST LIVING IN LOGAN SQUARE, *THE 1001 CHICAGO NIGHTS*, IS A COLLECTION OF ORIGINAL SHORT STORIES SET IN CHICAGO AND LOOSELY BASED ON THE CLASSIC, *1001 ARABIAN NIGHTS*. CENTERPIECE STORY, *ALI BABA AND THE FORTY THIEVES*, INTERWEAVES TWO OTHER LESSER-KNOWN ANCIENT TALES (*THE TALE OF OUJ, SON OF ANAK*, AND *TWO DUNCES, AND A THIRD*) TO SUPPORT THIS NOVELLA. UNLIKE THE ORIGINAL *NIGHTS*, WHICH INDEPENDENTLY STAND-ALONE OF EACH OTHER, THIS NOVELLA INTERLOCKS TWELVE ORIGINAL STORIES TOGETHER, CREATING A SINGLE STORY NOT PRESENT IN THE ARABIAN VERSION. THE COVER ART, TWO SNAILS SEATED SHELL TO SHELL, ARE A VISUAL ABSTRACT OF THE NUMERIC VALUE, 1001. THANK YOU AND PLEASE ENJOY, THE 1001 CHICAGO NIGHTS!

-YNA
NOVEMBER 2016

•••

THE
1001
CHICAGO NIGHTS

NOVELLA: ONE
by: yna

Two Drunkards and a Local Junky

John unlocked the door and saw a note taped to the register behind the bar.

"My brother needs to fix the place. Expect him around 5 but who knows with him", it read.

"Great! His brother starts rehab during happy hour, fucking great!" he thought of his boss' note.

Just as he waded it up, the bar door *crashed* open. John flinched so much he nearly dropped a load of shot glasses off the bar's edge. He thought the handyman arrived a little early, but it was not his boss' brother. Instead, he saw a large pair of silhouettes through the summer sunshine that radiated behind them.

Two Drunkards, an Artist, and a Musician sauntered over to the bar, like uncelebrated royalty, and ordered a round of cocktails. John knew they were drunk, he wasn't sure if they were there to collect a recent gambling debt. When the pair bragged about their hapless, yet loveable, Chicago baseball club it sounded all *too* familiar. He knew they weren't allied with the biker gang that held his debts, they were just drunk.

He'd some familiarity with the Illinois Dram Shop Act and didn't want to risk losing his night by night bartending job, *again.* Rather than serve them, he decided to eighty-six them, politely. After some moaning, the chunky fans of America's past-time collided into each other on their way out, getting jammed-up in the doorframe. They struggled to free themselves, grunting like a couple head of cattle stuck in the old stockyard. Once they did, they chimed-in a few slurs directed at John. He furrowed his brow and chuckled under his breath, "ha, ha, ha …

that's why I'm a fan of Chicago's *other* baseball team."

"Hey dudes ... uh, excuse me, gentlemen?" enquired a blonde woman, in black leather just outside the troublesome door. She was across the street on a stake out for her boss when she saw the pair go inside the bar. Thinking they might help her with some useful information regarding John's whereabouts, she stopped them.

"WHOA! Who are *you?*" the Artist replied. He thought her Biker looks were a sexy fashion statement and not reality.

"Uh, yea guy, you can check out my ass in these hot bitch pants, but is the bar dead inside?"

"I go clubbing til' 4am with clients on the Gold Coast and a hot chick, like *you,* has never approached me, nope. That's never happened to me, *ever...*" lamented the Artist.

"Well, how the fuck can you blame the ladies, lame ass. I mean really, man? Can't you see the lady needs a drink? Instead, you tell her how pathetic you are, revealing yourself too early and easily", snapped the Musician.

"*Oh*, you're right. I had no idea you needed a drink, ma'am. I'm so sorry that's what we're trying to do too and well …"

"Inside *that* bar, you know the one you just bounced out of … anyone inside?" demanded the Blonde.

Completely detached from her question as a pair of loose balloons drifting into the sky, the ambitious duo went on to explain to her all about the ballgame from earlier that afternoon. Then the Musician asked, "So, do you think they'll win it or just go to the Series?"

Before she could answer, they invited her again for some cocktails. She knew time was of the essence if she was going to track down John so she phrased it another way, "*Well!* You boys really had a full day, haven't you?"

Smitten to turn-on her charms as a master manipulator she placated their inner child while simultaneously massaging their male ego. She draped her arms over them and pulled them in real close, as if to huddle before she calmly said, "I'd just *love* to join you two boys, but until you can answer a question, I can't go anywhere with you – *Okay?*"

After briefly whining about the terms of their arrangement, the two agreed to answer her question. "So then," she began, "did either of you talk to a guy named *John?* Any guy named John, inside *that* bar?" she methodically asked, pointing her long index finger toward the bar. Neither responded, but looked puzzled instead.

"Uh, he's tall … blue eyes, dirty-blonde hair. He might be tending bar, anyone like that inside?" Again, she gestured toward the bar and waited. Looking bewildered by her question, the Musician spoke up, " *Why?* Is he your boyfriend or something?"

"Please excuse my rude friend, ma'am. I did not see anyone inside. In fact the bartender is a real JERK!" the Artist yelled toward the bar.

The Blonde crossed her arms and smiled, she knew only John could be so annoying that even drunkards would leave his bar spitting mad. The two proceeded to lob curses at the building, the bar, and its' tender before she asked, "So, nobody very important is inside that nasty bar, huh boys?"

"Well, uh… I'm not so sure, now. I might have seen a guy shooting pool, way in the back," the Musician explained.

"*Huh?*" the confused Artist said.

"Uh, yea dude there was one guy way in the back."

"What? I don't think so, I didn't see any… wait, that's right, we *did* see some guy … shooting pool was it?"

"Right, shooting pool," the Musician tried to explain, but she saw through their flimsy coordinated lie.

"So, besides the bartender you saw one other guy, is that right?"

"Right," the Artist confirmed.

"We could invite him for a drink. What'd ya say we treat you to a drink instead of him?" the Musician suggested.

"A drink, *where* … this bar?" she asked, gesturing at the bar.

"At *this* bar? Of course not at *this* bar, at another bar just down the street here", the Artist proposed. Rather on cue, the Musician slid his arm around her waist and quickly led her down the sidewalk. The Blonde who was not at all interested in drinking, smiled, pretending to go along as they led her down Milwaukee Avenue.

Nearly passing a liquor store, the Drunkards couldn't resist the urge for a couple flasks of vodka, to help, "… keep the buzz going." She insisted to wait outside for a smoke and after slapping high-fives, she patted them on their butts before she sparked it up. She watched her smoke drift, like a lost ghost, into the street before a passing 56 CTA bus whisked it into the soupy air. At about that time, she saw her drinking buddies inside the store guzzling liquid cheddar straight from the dispenser at the nacho machine. She quickly abandoned the drunken duo by slipping into a near-by cab and vanishing away into the city.

When the Drunkards emerged to find her gone, they stomped down the sidewalk then romped from bar to bar searching for her. Instead, they found some neighborhood artist installation party. After a couple shots to appreciate the skewed artwork, they moved on, as she was not on display at the artist's show. On their way out, both respectfully hocked loogies on the sidewalk in front of the bar.

It was well into the evening when the creative hi-brows stumbled down Cortland Street to a near-by party. They learned of this party from a couple girls they ran into at Club Luca, while searching for the Blonde. On their way to the revelry, they pulled out the flasks for a pleasant stroll beneath the orange glow of city streetlights. The Musician took a gluttonous gulp of vodka, winced as it dropped into his stomach, and said, "In addition to imbibing these spirits, why don't we bide our time together by each of us wishing for something we want … uh, **burp** besides another drink."

"Well vocalized, you fine crooner," concurred the Artist. "I'll start by yearning to be adored. I wish for fate to send me a large collection of admirers who exult me as if I'm Michelangelo, and everything I create is The David. In this way, I supplement my preexisting artistic ability with what I lack now, wealth, and fame."

"*And I,*" sang the jealous Musician, "*find you to be a revolting sell-out, or more of a talentless comedian than an artist!*"

"Hey! Shut the hell up down there ya drunk, bums", growled an unseen voice from an open window above the sidewalk where they roamed.

"I wish", whispered the Musician, "that fate send a collection of cynical critics to assail your creative monstrosities, as a wolf devours sheep, tearing each one limb from limb until your work is no more!"

"Whoa there big, bad wolf, but I fail to recognize this highly offensive joke as a sign of our friendship. Is this the reward I get for loyal companionship as we imbibe these fine spirits?"

Somewhere near the bridge at Cortland and Elston, the pair squabbled, shouted, and finally came to blows, but not before diligently securing their respective flasks behind a garbage bin, bursting with trash. After some flailing and occasionally rolling about the filthy, wet ground, the Artist barfed first. Most landed on the Musician, including a few chunks of partially digested hot dog from the ballgame earlier in the day. Then smelling the sour spew, the Musician blew chunks, too. Despite wearing their respective regurgitations, they brawled until thoroughly exhausted.

After a brief respite for air, they mutually agreed to make the next person to pass over the near-by bridge an umpire between them. The wager: winner takes both vodka flasks and what was left of their pride.

As it happened, the first person to come their way was an old junky who was also familiar with the neighborhood. He pushed a rusted shopping cart loaded with various sorts of rubbish when they stopped and asked him to be referee between them.

After the local Junky, turned ad hoc judge, heard what they wanted, he shook his head, as would any reflective and respectable magistrate. Then, without remark, he slowly bent down to retrieve two small vials of heroin he'd tucked into his dirty sock. His hands trembled when he picked the flasks out of the trash bin. He brought the flasks and vials to the bridge's edge and emptied their respective contents into the dreary Chicago River below.

Stunned, the Drunkards looked on, bewildered by his actions. Turning to them to hand them their property, the empty flasks, the Junky asked, "Pardon me, saucy pair of pickled pigs' ass, but is there any honey in these bottles?"

"*No,*" they replied, baffled by his query.

"There never was any honey in *these* bottles, you absurd Junky", screamed the Musician.

"Nor were there ever any brains in your empty heads!" rebuked the Junky, turned street Judge, as he stumbled away pushing his cart toward Wicker Park.

●●●

Le Soirée Dérangé

They watched the Junky pass under the Cortland via duct when the Musician hollered, "*Hey you*! You're a fucking junky bum, you know *that!*"

The Junky shouted back just as a Metra train passed overhead.

"What's he saying now?" the Artist asked.

"Who the fuck knows, the train's drowning his dumb-ass out." Despite being filthy with muddy barf, they had no intention to miss an opportunity for late night debauchery.

"It's this way, dude."

"No, it's *inside* the metal foundry", the Musician explained.

"What's that *smack, smack*", the Artist licked his lips and asked, "What's that metallic taste? It's coming from the foundry, dude, are you sure we should…"

"Would you shut the fuck up and just follow me before I bitch slap you like I did before that decrepit Junky shithead."

"Fuck you, don't talk to me that way."

They bickered in between coughing through the foundry's web of cobblestone streets that coiled around like intestines. Sulfur particles from the smelting process bathed their lungs with every inhalation along their path. Hidden around a corner, behind a belching steam grate, they found it. Converted from a foundry warehouse, it had a well-manicured garden and appeared as any suburban mansion. Allured by such peculiar paradox, they were anxious to explore the decadence that surely awaited them.

Outside in the garden, some guests smoked various leafy green products, mostly tobacco. Others lazily lay on chaise lounge chairs enjoying flavored vapors from giant hookah water pipes.

To get inside they passed through a pair of large steel doors that opened into a candle lit foyer. A ten-foot black velvet drape separated the foyer from the main party room, their crucible. They lustfully stretched to draw the curtain when something suddenly yanked them backward.

"Where the fuck do you think you're going?" a bouncer asked, grabbing the pair by their collars.

"Excuse me?" asked the Artist.

"I said, do you have an invitation?" The Bouncer was bulky and strong as anyone might expect. A black leather vest exposed her tattoo-blanketed arms, while a well-groomed, pink Mohawk crested the top of her head.

"An invitation?" the Musician asked, brushing her hand off his collar.

"Oh no, we were told about this party by a couple very attractive ladies at a nearby club," explained the Artist.

"Is that right?"

"Sure is", boasted the Musician, "one had purple hair and…"

"And the other is a redhead. I don't remember their names, do you?" asked the Artist of his affiliate.

"Names…? They never gave us any fuck'n names they just told us where it was, man. I've been to plenty of afterhours parties just like this one, what's the problem?" the Musician said as he lit-up a cigarette with a chrome zippo. The butane flame flared in his eyes before he haughtily slapped it shut.

"Sorry, that's not enough for this kind of party", she flatly rejected.

They had to know what was behind the curtain; they had to get inside to find out, so the Artist asked, "What else did they say? Something about, *uh*, have a great night. *Uh*, come to a swank party, or what was it?"

"What was where?"

"No you idiot, what did they say?"

"What did who say?"

"Did you lose your brain in the Chicago River? What did…".

"The chicks … what did the hot biker chicks with the colorful hair tell you?" the Bouncer interrupted, refreshing his memory.

"They said there was a swank party here and we should show up for a wild time tonight and get some spectacular scrambled eggs in the morning, or some sexy shit like that, I think."

"No, wait. They said we'd have a wild night, a good morning, and … uh, a spectacular afternoon", the Artist suddenly recalled with a smile.

She frowned, sniffed their eau du spew, then eyeballing their mucked-up baseball regalia, calmly responded, "Alright. That's it."

"What's it?"

"That's it, your both in."

"We are? We're in?

"Those special lady friends of yours gave you permission to enter this evening's soiree. I have no choice, I have to let you in, bonsoir Monsieur", she said then pulled back the heavy black velvet drapes, letting them pass. "See stupid-ass. I knew how to get us in", the Artist, whispered to the Musician as they quickly entered.

Beyond the black drapes, it opened into a massive warehouse like no other party either had ever seen. The social norm was dancing, drinking, smoking, snorting, or any combination thereof. Guests indulged their choice of weed, cocaine, crystal meth, crack, or heroin among other pill-popping varieties. Formal servers handed out the beer, wine, and morsels while serving top-shelf liquors on demand. Though clothing was worn, typically black leather, a dress code hardly mattered as some guests exposed more than tans lines from Oak Street Beach.

"Cats or rats, rats or cats, take your pick, place your bet", the Artist heard a nearby concessioner hock, so he asked him about his proposition.

"All the action's in the basement. You can place a bet with me or downstairs", he replied.

"So there is betting going on? Gambling, like on craps and cards?" the Musician confirmed with the bookie-concessioner.

"Right, all the tables are downstairs, too."

"So you're booking bets on a dog fight or a cat fight?"

"Neither. Its cats against rats, they're in the pit downstairs", he said motioning toward a stairwell in a far corner of the warehouse. The duo bickered over who'd win, then placed their respective bets with the concessioner. However, before they made it to the pit to watch the cruelty, something colorful drew the Artist's attention to the bar.

"Holy shit, how did they get here so fast? It's them, the chicks are here."

"Where, I don't see any … shit, you're right. Who's that dude they're with?"

"Now, how am I supposed to know that? Hmm, but they don't seem to be interested in … ok, now they're touching him", the Artist noticed.

"Ok, that's it, let's go say, hello", the Musician jealously insisted. With vodka martinis in hand, they strode into a pool of perspiring partiers. They weaseled their way next to the man who was with the girls and waited, and waited, and waited to see if the girls recognized them but alas, they did not. The girls were far too interested in the man to care. Indeed, this bruised their pride but it was what happened next that summoned their anger.

As they waited to be noticed, they over-heard the Purplehead tell the man, "…its upstairs, totally private and fun, Joey. It will be like going to a restricted party, within a secret party, right? So, once we get you there uh…"

"Ooo, once we get you upstairs, Joey, we'll have some fucking fun", the Redhead finished her Purpleheaded partner's thoughts then slid her right hand down the man's pants and stroked his cock. When the Artist saw this, he became angry and slammed his martini on the bar.

"Well…. Hello there," he said. "And, how are you two doing tonight? Quite a party you invited us to."

"Hey, you guys made it here, great!" the Redhead said as she quickly removed her hand from his pants. "Glad to see you guys made it," she said, extending the same hand for a shake.

"I wouldn't touch that hand until she washed it, Bro," the Musician advised before he asked, "Who's the dude with you?"

"Uh, he's a friend of ours. His name is Joe and he…"

"Joe! pleasure da meet ya'," the Musician interrupted. He put his arm over Joe and explained, "So nice of you to give us a little time first, you know?"

"What did you just say to our guest?" The Purplehead asked.

"Your guest...? We thought you invited us."

"Sir, if there's a problem, I can..." the man began.

"Joe, there's no need to respond to these rude and presumptuous drunkards. They're lucky we invited them at all after they *ran* into us earlier."

"Listen up, strawberry pie. You and your friend invited us, and we just want...

"So what! If you expected more than our invitation, too fucking bad, go fuck yourself in the men's room!" the Purplehead screamed at the Musician.

"Is everything alright over here?" asked a leather-clad brunette biker standing next to them.

"Yea, I think so. We're just…"

"No, it's not alright," the Musician butted in, before sipping his martini and continuing. "We're having a conversation over here that you're interrupting with your intrusive concerns. So, why don't you mind your girlfriend, tough guy, and put a top on your puppy."

Silent dread came to rest upon them all, for the Musician's insult was so arrogant and haughty it shamed misogynists. The Brunette invited her date earlier that night while visiting a local strip club. She saw her date strip, liked what she saw, and wanted her to join in the soiree as her guest. Her guest was a petite size C and proved it publicly, as her open vest exposed her endowments, quite well. Now, the Brunette's pride was offended and her petite guests' feelings hurt.

Across the dance floor was the Blonde that the Drunkards encountered earlier that evening. She laughed with her boss, the biker gang Captain, as they bragged about collecting Johns' gambling debt. "And then, did you see his face when I called him a, 'chiseler', I thought he was gon'a shit in fear!" Suddenly, the sound of shattering glass broke their happy conversation. When she looked up, the Blonde said, "Holy shit, it can't be them. Un-fucking-real, they won't go away. I'll take care of this problem, Boss," before her Boss knew what happened, she was half-way across the warehouse.

"Hey! That was my cocktail! You must replace my martini immediately."

"Oh yea, well go fuck yourself and your buddy for disparaging us with your lifestyle judgments. In fact, let me show you just how I feel...."

As the Brunette reached for a small shank buried in her pocket, the Blonde wedged between them, as a crafty referee.

"Boy's, welcome!" she declared. "So glad you could join our petite soirée this evening.

"Well, where the fuck have you been?" demanded the Musician.

"Holy shit, you're the hostess? Did you know she just knocked a vodka martini out of my hands? Top shelf no less," explained the Artist.

"Oh my, I'm so sorry. Here, why don't I replace that for you, and…"

She immediately replaced the martini then poured three shots of vodka. While they weren't looking, she signaled to an underling who led them away. The Purple and Red heads with their guest slipped behind the bar where they disappeared through a secret passage.

"*Sante!*" The Blonde shouted, raising her shot glass with the Drunkards. After she woofed her shot, she leaned over and whispered to the Brunette, "why don't you take your lady friend outside, and wait there, I've got some special plans for our guests here. Follow, silently."

Understanding her instructions, the Brunette quietly led her topless guest outside. "That's right we're supposed to be here! That's right!" the Drunkards berated the couple.

The Blonde smacked their dirty chests, and said, "Hey, their leaving, now. Leave them alone."

"Right, their leaving," agreed the Artist "What a peculiar party to see you at? So, how have you been since we last saw you?"

"I'm fine, but did you two roll around in some mud or something?"

"Oh yea, we got into a little scrape on the way over here", the Musician explained.

"You got into a fight, huh? So, tell me the other guys got it worse than you, right?"

"Uh, it was us. We got into a fight … with each other."

"Huh, imagine that."

"Yea, well you know sometimes that sort of thing happens and men like us, well, we have to take care of …."

"Hey! Do you want some fun? I mean some real fuckin' fun!" she burst out. To make up for her misgivings from earlier in the evening, when she ditched them on Milwaukee Avenue, she promised to escort them to an alternate party herself in an SUV limousine parked outside. The astute Blonde led them to believe this was the very party they would find Joe and the girls at, so naturally, they agreed to go along.

ꙮ

A Random John

The Junky heard their taunts and shouted back, "You can lick the ass of a goddess but she'll still shit all over you, you drunken dunces!" After shouting back, he realized the roaring Metra train probably drowned out his curse. "Aaaah, Fuck it," he mumbled, before pushing on to Wicker Park.

As he made his way, a metallic brown sedan screeched sharply out of a valet parking lot in front of the Green Ferry Lounge and onto Damen Avenue. He dodged the reckless roadster, flexing his legs over his cart, nearly kissing the polished chrome bumper with his ass.

"*Hey, hey ...* you got' a better mouth, man!" the Junky howled incoherently as it tore down North Avenue. The sedans' screeching tires sprayed smoky black bits of rubber across his face that lodged in his beard. A crowd stared as he hastily tried to brush and pick the pieces off before he trudged through the gawkers.

Ultra-violet sparks belched from the 'L's third rail at the Damen stop and drifted down, falling like crumbs from an electric meal. He bounced in cadence to the rhythmic drums thumping inside Two Door Liquors live show. His veins throbbed with the need, the same synergistic spirit that possessed the place and attracted so many spirts cavorting in the flesh.

Then, somewhere under the outstretched track between Damen and the Wood Street tunnel, he saw something. Sweat drizzled into his eyes through crevasses on his dirt-crusted brow. Squinting into the dark distance, he saw a tiny light bounce about the alley then, it quickly rolled into the blackest shadow, disappearing behind some city garbage bins. He stopped, blinked and rubbed his eyes then looked again but it was gone. He saw nothing but a well-beaten path below the tracks.

"Hey ... hey buddy, ya' lookin for something?" a familiar voice from within the darkness called to him. He stared below the tracks, but saw only darkness until, into a beam of cloudy street light emerged a skinny pair of alabaster legs. Her loose fitting fishnet stockings were perched atop a pair of strappy four-inch heels. A Hooker, with bedraggled, dirty blonde hair greeted him with a smile forged from thick red lips and heavy, blue eye shadow. In a tiny black bikini top, she smacked her bubble gum as if it was sticky mouthwash.

"*Well,* honey …" she sassily said before she lifted her seven-inch scarlet skirt, to push her well-groomed goods. While she did her best to market herself, the Junky simply stared in her direction and said nothing. He squinted behind her, peering into the darkness to see if anything … any anomaly or some irregular movement … but there was nothing, no bouncing balls of light.

"Look Sweetie, the street lights go dim in a couple hours, aw'right!" she laughed coarsely, coughing up a mouth full of phlegm before spitting. She fully expected him to laugh, or at least chuckle at her jokes, but he did not. When she saw this, she demanded, "Are you fucking ignoring me, you douche bag … *now,* I'm getting pissed off you fuck'n, limp dick!" she shouted, before turning around to grab her ankles.

Over the years the two became somewhat acquainted by their mutual love for torment, misery, and heroin. She knew about him … all about him, for good or bad. The first time it happened was years earlier after a night of drinking at Two Door Liquors, the small venue where the Stones, among other greats, poured their spirit all over the stage. He was employed and drinking happily with friends after they enjoyed a local band. He was a junior associate at Kerkfield and Alice, making six figures and partying with colleagues when not busy logging billable hours. Ralph was his name back then, and he had many friends and lots of money. Around midnight, after the cabaret show, they called a Uryder for a ride home. They all wanted to be in the office early Saturday morning to work and not nurse a hangover. As the driver passed Wicker Park, Ralph saw them – fluorescent green balls of light, floating about.

He screamed, *"Stop! Stop the car!"*, so he could point them out to his fellow associates.

"Uh, there's a lot of traffic here, Sir. Maybe we should…" the driver said.

"Now, look ... look there, right there! What is that, holy shit?" he shouted after jumping out of the back seat and into Damen Avenue traffic.

"Excuse me, Sir, get back in the car!" shouted the driver but Ralph ignored him. "I'm sorry ma'am, but I cannot possibly give you a five star rating, now!" declared the driver to one of Ralph's colleagues when the first horn echoed through the night.

Though he saw them, none of his friends did. They said to him, "... you're nuts! Get back in the car, Ralphie! You're gon'a get yourself killed!"

"Look! What is that? Look ... You can't see that, not one of you? Can't anybody see them!" he screamed at passers-by. Only car horns and the irate responded, except for one voice that peeped above all the noisy confusion into his keen ears.

"Mister, are you talking about the green lights over there in the park? Sure, I can see them over there. You can see them too, huh?" replied a skinny, disheveled, and dirty looking girl standing next to him. He looked down at her and so began their friendship, love affair, and addiction.

The scene created a giant traffic jam, to the ire of the Uryder driver among others. Ralph's colleagues tried to coax him back into the car, but before their lawyerly efforts could lure him back in, he ran off with the skinny, dirty girl, treading through traffic and away from a career. The driver and his friends drove on rather than risk causing a riot. Within a month, he lost his job, as tales of "Ralph's Uryder incident" penetrated his life like a venereal disease. After that, he slid into a bottle of binge boozing before becoming a full-time drunkard *then* devolving into heroin junky.

Though many doctors' worked with him, their words echoed in Ralph's head with meaningless, spite. "Now, Ralph no one can see strange objects that aren't actually there, and everyone has a bad day, right?" He gave the right answer to the doctors, but to him, their well-intended advice was *not* synonymous with reality as *he* experienced it.

Then, as if on cue, she bent over and spread her small cheeks to plug her goods for the hard sell. The Hooker reached between her legs and gently stroked her kitty until it purred. She wiped up her sugar and smeared it over her tongue, like vanilla icing on her finger. She sucked on it until it was good and clean, then calmly gestured to him to come closer from between her spindly legs.

The Junky, who couldn't help but notice her primal seduction, enjoyed the idea of mixing his addiction with his good old, same old girl. Ready to jump in, he took one-step toward her open enticement when, suddenly, he saw something dart about behind her. He stopped and peered into the dark distance under the elevated tracks… then it moved again!

"No, no … *NO!* Get *away!* Get the fuck away right now!" he screamed. The Junky staggered, nearly becoming just another man falling backward into the gutter. Just before falling, he caught himself on his heavy shopping cart and slowly meandered toward Wicker Park, mumbling curses along Damen Avenue.

"Hey … *hey*, man! … Fuck you, man, *shit*!" she hollered from between her legs, watching him walk away upside down. She stood up and fixed her skirt about her tiny waist, before lamenting, "What the fuck does a girl have to do around here to get some dude to fuck her! *Shit!* Come on now. Fuck … my ass is pretty, isn't it?" Then she peeked over her shoulder to admire her skinny, little ass.

At about that time, another shopper appeared and slowly drifted from the dark, into a shadow near-by. He spotted her looking for her own butt beneath the pale streetlight. This particular random john heard her impassioned laments from the darkness under the elevated, perking his interests.

"Are you looking for something?"

"*Hey* … where the fuck'd *you* come from?"

"Oh, not too far away, sort of near-by, depending upon your perception of space and the time it takes to get from one place to another", he replied, as he passed beneath the street light. The Well-dressed man was tall, clean-shaven with jet-black hair, slicked back and shiny. His dark, inset eyes drew the Hooker in, so she responded, "Uh … yea, I sure did lose something… you wanna help me find it, buddy?!" she gagged after she stumbled to turn around on her four inch heels.

"Fuck, I don't know what the problem was with that *other* guy? One minute, ya' think you got'a friend and the next minute he's… he's runn'in off into the night", she said, gesturing toward the park. Her eyes bordered on the outskirts of the truth and the Well-dressed man knew it.

"Huh? Imagine that. The poor ignorant chap fanatically serves his master, causing him to overlook you, ma'am", he said, tipping his head down and toward her.

"Yea, well he's a little prick who loves pricks in his arm when he should have a prick shoved up his fuck'in..."

"Ah, yes the various acts of sex. Precisely, what I wanted to discuss with you, ma'am. Why, I'm sure we could arrange something like that with a sexy woman like you, correct?"

"Oh well thank you, sir. But, trust me buddy, there's nothing here I haven't sucked, fucked, or gotten off some other fuckin' way, *aw'right*!" she cackled, grabbing her crotch then licking her middle finger. She carefully sucked on the tip before extending her salute, with a smile. "Yea ... that's right! A ticket to ride *my train* ain't cheap, *buddy*", she said.

"*Well,* I should get down to business then", he proposed, reaching into his inner coat pocket. He pulled out a tightly wrapped roll of crisp hundred-dollar bills, bound by a thick crimson rubber band. He slipped the roll over her extended middle finger, like a ring and said, "Here you are then. *This,*" he said, "should be enough to take care of my needs for the night. There are exactly eleven Benny's there, you can do the math yourself, correct?" Then, he nonchalantly sauntered out of the smoky street light and back into the shadows under the tracks.

The Hooker was stunned to the point of silence. Usually, she'd tell a random john something like, "*Oh yea ...* you'll have to do a lot better than that, *limp dick!*" before flicking her cigarette at him. That was usually enough to scare them off or, alternately, get them to cough up more cash. However, she knew this john was different, "*a hundred, what the fuck? It's more than, a thousand and what? This spiffy mother fucker is fuckin' crazy*", she thought, before blurting out.

"*Woo!* Sure I can go with you to the show tonight! Let's go in through the backdoor, sexy man. You are a very sexy man, ya' know that? Hey, can I call you Benny?" Then, she jumped into the darkness to catch a ride with her uncommon, yet, random john.

BEWARE THE PARK AFTER DARK

Their whispers rode upon a breeze that blew across the park. The sound entered his ears as he approached from the Damen Blue Line stop. When the Junky looked up, he saw four or five tiny glowing globules float about the fountain in front of the field house. With a deep breathe he calmly rolled his shopping cart up the nearest alley, behind the old Pontiac Taproom. He quickly rummaged through his cart for a special empty brass jar, hidden inside an old wooden box. He stealthily snuck across the street to the park, his hunter's heart thumped with anticipation.

Nearby, Joe, the baker, closed shop for the night. He lived and worked in Wicker Park for nearly ten years and was working late that night to fill an order for the next day. It was on his way home that night when something happened that changed his life, for eternity.

At first, he saw someone running in the park and thought little of it. It was late night and things like that were typical in the neighborhood. Then, as he watched from the sidewalk, Joe saw him squat, as if to hide, along the steps at the base of the fountain.

"What the hell is that guy doing?" thought Joe. In the blink of an eye, the Junky jumped from his crouched position, and bounded across the fountain's plaza, leaping with his brass jar into the air. He dropped to the ground and rolled himself into a ball around the fountain. There, he stayed entirely still, for a few moments, until he popped back up. He was trying to catch what looked like fireflies to curious Joe. Astonished by the orchestra of lights that danced about, Joe stopped to watch. He shook his head and rubbed his tired eyes, thinking perhaps, he was so tired that his bleary eyes must be lying to him. That

didn't help, so to validate his own perception, Joe looked for witnesses. He saw three young men walking toward him so when they got close, Joe asked them, "Pardon me, but what are those lights in the park ... the ones that are over by the fountain?"

Puzzled by such a question and drunk anyway the three casually looked into the dark park, toward the fountain. When Joe pointed them out, they slowly looked, long and attentively enough to shake their heads before they kept walking. Joe frowned, but did not bother to ask them again. He figured they were drunk and simply could not see what was so obvious to him. Instead, he continued to watch the orbs evade their predator through the fountains' spray, spinning high into the black city sky before diving back down into the water.

Busses, cabs, cars all passed by, but none seemed to notice the light show over the fountain. Perplexed, Joe waited on the sidewalk and watched until he saw two young women. Dressed in black leather, one was a red head, and the other had dyed purple hair. The girls, who were each in their early twenties, might have ignored Joe and the lights all together, but for Joe, who hysterically asked them, "Uhh, excuse me... uhh, I'm sure this sounds strange, but do either of you happen to see that guy jumping around in the park?"

They looked and both replied, "Yep, we see him."

"Ok, good. So, what is he doing besides running around, jumping?"

"Uh, looks like he's losing his mind over there," the Redhead said.

"Yea, that or he's trying to find it somewhere over there in the park?" the Purplehead guessed.

"Uh, no," Joe responded. "Neither of you see him chasing those lights in the park, near the fountain?"

The girls stopped giggling and politely looked into the darkness of the park, and then looked at each other. After a brief pause, one girl shook her head and replied, "Do you mean the street lights around the park?"

"No, no, no. There, over there ... see, that guy near the fountain jumping around trying to catch the lights?" he explained. Again, the young women confirmed that they saw the Junky jumping around the fountain with an empty jar, cursing at lights that no one, apparently, could see.

"Neither of you can see the lights moving around? You can see that guy there, but you can't see the lights he's chasing. *Look now!* Did you see that, *there?* Look at that red one, what's it doing? What the hell *is* that?

The Redhead in braids stood on the tiptoes of her stilettos looking for the lights, but simply frowned and shook her head. Then the Purplehead stretched as high as her army boots would lift her to look. When she finished looking, she starred at the Redhead, giggled, before each burst out laughing. Then, without saying a word to Joe, they just walked away down the sidewalk snickering.

"Hey, you don't see them... you *really* don't see them?" Joe exclaimed as the girls strolled away from the park.

Joe was desperate to find out if someone else could see the lights, so he decided to confront the Junky himself. He crossed the park and slowly walked up the steps to the fountain's plaza, where the Junky was jumping to catch a green glowing orb. Just as he captured it inside his jar, Joe quietly crept up behind him and said, "Pardon me, sir, I..."

"*AHHHH!* What the...!" screamed the Junky. He bobbled then fumbled and dropped the brass jar onto the hard granite ground that surrounded the fountain. The beautiful orb blissfully bounced back into the summer's night. Then, like a spooked flock of pigeons, they all flew off, into the starry sky.

"No, NO, *NOOO!!!* Come back! Come back here you little, mother fuckers! *NOOO!*"

The Junky leapt from the fountains' platform and sprinted across the public lawn screaming at the lights that sped away into the night. Soon, he flopped onto the cool green grass, completely limp from disappointment. Joe came running up to him as he lay still in the grass. Suddenly, he jumped up and launched into a vicious verbal tirade, "What the *fuck* is wrong with you? Who walks up behind someone else in the middle of the fucking night, in a park, and scares the *fuck* out of them like that, HUH?! ... WHO?!"

Joe shook his head not able to speak. The Junky waited for an answer and when one was not forthcoming fast enough, he responded, "Well, let's keep it simple. Who the fuck are you, huh? To what do I owe this fucking honor, huh?"

"Uh, I was just walking home and, I, I saw you hiding by the fountain. And then,"

"Yea, and then what, huh?" screamed the Junky. "Did you think you'd come fuck with me to prove some point?!"

"Well, I saw you chasing after those lights or orbs or whatever those things are. You *can* see them, right?"

The Junky frowned then slowly walked straight up to Joe, and looked directly into his eyes. He tilted his head left, then right, examining his eyes carefully. "Huh?" he scoffed. Then he turned around and walked into the park with his arms extended outward and said, "Well, well, well you never know what you'll find here in the park after dark, I guess. Huh, **wow**, what the *fuck*?"

"Wait... no, I'm sorry. I really didn't mean to scare you. I just..."

"Oh, don't worry you don't scare me, *you parasite*! You didn't scare me at all but really, who the fuck sneaks up behind someone in the middle of a park ... at night, *huh?*! What freak does that? Why aren't *you* fucking crazy if you can see the same thing I can, *huh?*"

"Look, I'm sorry" pleaded Joe, but before he could ask the Junky any questions, there was a loud bang from a city garbage can, near the dog run area. Both men watched the thirty gallon drum rattle and shake before it tipped over, seemingly by itself. The Junky grabbed his jar, its lid, and gave chase to a couple orbs that hid inside that no one else could see. Suddenly, he stopped and turned, "*YOU!*" he screamed and pointed at Joe who watched the lights zip low across the lawn.

"You can scare me once, but you better leave me alone from now on! I work alone, you got it, you crazy night crawling, jackass!" the Junky shouted then, ran across the park and into the night, his silhouette exposed to Joe's eyes by the lights he chased in the dark distance.

⁂

SOME WICKED PAYBACK

John poured shots of whiskey for his crew as he explained why booking bets through him gave them better odds to win, when the door *SLAMMED* open. The jukebox skipped a beat as the door hit the wall, startling John so much, he drizzled some whiskey on his black button-down. He rolled his eyes and huffed before standing upright at six foot, four inches tall. The humming window unit broke the awkward stillness through the bar before he bellowed, "I thought I told you chuckleheads to get the hell out of …"

He thought the Drunkards returned for happy hour, but when he turned around, he realized his mistake. He saw their black silhouettes eclipse the sunlight blazing through the bar's entry. Flanked by her blonde lieutenant, the Captain marched directly to the bar. To shelter his greedy pride, John ran to meet them at the far end of the bar away from his crew of bettors.

"Hey… has our money arrived, yet?" she asked. John shook his head and calmly said, "No, not exactly, but I can explain, uh, just not during work. You know it *is* happy hour and…"

"Uh-huh, I see", said the Captain as she stroked her chin. "Well then, when will it get here?"

"The money – oh, like I said, it's happy hour right now, and so can I get you a…"

"Oh *really,* you're working, making some money right now."

"Uhh …" John gulped under the quick questioning to take stock of the interrogatory. "Yes, I am so…. What can I get for you?"

"We're wondering where our money is. You said you'd pay us last week but *here* we are this week. We don't care about your explanation we just care about our money. You cared about the money when you asked to borrow it, but now you don't care? *So*, I'll politely ask you again … where's our fucking money?"

Though the bar had an air conditioner that kept it cool in Chicago's late summer heat, John began to sweat big thick drops that rolled down his back. His eyes fluttered, nearly falling over from fright, and then confidently reiterated, "I really have no way to pay you right now because I'm working, but I'd love to buy you two ladies a couple cocktails, beers, or shots?"

"So it's about you working. You work for money, is that correct?"

John affirmed with a nod and leaned closer.

"So you have money, because you're working, right?

Again, he nodded and politely smiled.

"But you can't pay us because … you're working? Well, that sounds flaky to me. How 'bout you?" She turned to the Blonde who bluntly replied, "Chipy, he's trying to chisel us."

"Nah, you think so? I don't think he's that dumb, do you? Watch, I'll ask him," then she turned back to him to ask, "You chiseling me? Are you a chiseler?"

John shook his head, denying the charge. He tried to explain that he was not a chiseler, but it was too late. She was not amused, but smiled anyway when she leaned over the bar and grabbed him by his collar. The happy hour crowd of bettors stopped mid-drink to watch. She pulled him over the bar, real close to her face and very clearly, spoke, "We're not fucking around with you, why are *you* fucking around with *us?*"

John's lips parted when he felt his feet lift gently off the ground from her brute forte. He was speechlessly hanging on for her next move when she asked, "How you feelin' now, huh? Feel like giving us the fucking cash so you can get back to *work?*"

The stench of her rotting teeth wafted into his face and up his nostrils, causing him to gag. He stuttered with dry-mouth, "I, I have to get it. I, I'd be happy to, uhh, do that, let me go and I'll get it."

She let him go and he hustled over to the chrome register where he kept his backpack. He nervously unzipped it and reached inside. His buddies watched him scuttle from the opposite end of the bar and grab the wad of cash he collected from them moments earlier.

He quietly handed it to her and calmly but firmly said, "*Now*", his voice strained as he straightened out his shirt collar, "can I get either of you ladies a happy hour cocktail?" His pride hoped to restore his image to his pals by serving the bikers a round. She carefully examined the wad then counted it out on the bar as her lieutenant watched over her shoulder.

When she'd finished indulging her greed, and was happy, she tapped the length of the stacked cash on the bar and said, "No… no, thank you. I think we'll be going now. Thanks for the cash. See you in a couple weeks, buddy, keep working hard for that cheese." He leaned against the bar with both arms extended anxiously watching them exit. Then, like a true showman, he looked to the far end of the bar where his buds silently stared back.

"Aw'right, Aw'right", he said, grabbing a bottle of Kentucky bourbon from the top shelf. "Who's booking the bets down here, and who's the dumb ass that thought I'd get my ass kicked, huh?!"

Before they had time to laugh at him, the bar door *banged* open again. This time, he spilled the bottle all over the bar and onto his buddies instead of their shot glasses. He nervously thought his debt collectors had returned for some extra interest, but he was wrong.

"So sorry I'm late, rush hour traffic is a real pain in the ass, right now. I just dropped a ride off at O'Hare and hustled back here to start work", the handyman said. A six-foot ladder draped over his shoulder hit the metal doorframe when he came in.

"Yea, I know," John used a damp hand towel to clean up the bourbon. "Great, no problem, but I can't let you start work down here, Al. It's happy hour and as you can see, there are some patrons here. I know Bubba told you to work in the bar, but why don't you just start upstairs, man, and come down here when we're closed?"

"What? I could've kept rolling until then. *Fuck*, he needs to figure that out before having me come in so early" Al replied. "Fine, let me get my stuff and I'll work upstairs until closing. You're closing at 2am, right?"

John nodded as he re-poured the shots, ignoring Al who adjourned upstairs. Al was not rich, but he took pride in being humble. He was born and raised in one of the many, less-fortunate neighborhoods of Chicago, where he and his fraternal twin-brother, Bubba (adapted from his proper name, "Burhan") were raised by their parents, Ishmael and Layla. The Qizil's (shortened from Qizilbash, or "redheads") were a poor family but what little inheritance their parents left for them they shared more or less. Beyond that, the brothers shared little else, including appearance; Bubba had hazel eyes and red curly hair, Al had dark eyes and straight black hair.

However, the most significant difference between them was their respective wealth. Growing up, Bubba worked hard as a stock boy at a local liquor and beer distributorship, eventually working his way up to general manager. After fifteen years of hard work, he became wealthy enough to purchase the distributorship among other investment property. He bought an elegant home on Kedzie Boulevard where he hoped to begin a family. For years, he paid his brother to be caretaker and repairman of his properties. Al inherited their parents' home in west Logan Square. Al delivered the Sun Times as a kid, pizzas as a teenager, and people in a taxicab as a man. However, since buying a newer car he chose to drive for Uryder, under the Illinois Ride Sharing Act, instead. He liked the freedom to make his own hours and driving his own car to make money for payments on it.

Sweat quickly soaked through his clothes, carrying his gear to the third floor. Without air conditioning, the top floor baked in the sun so he opened all the windows as a beacon to a breeze. He set up his gear and got straight to work, dispensing of anger at his brother into labor. He worked steadily through the night until one in the morning. Then, he needed a break so he ambled through a large wooden framed window and on to the rusted fire escape for a smoke break.

Bolted to the masonry of the building was a fire escape that wrapped around the building's exterior. The iron archeological site hovered over thirty feet above the alleyway in the back of the building. A gentle breeze lapped at his drenched clothing, cooling him like an evaporative air conditioner. He lit up a smoke and before long, his tired feet begged for a respite. He sat down on the escape, propping his feet up on its rail when out of the blackness of the night streaked a star with a long greenish-blue tail…. He smirked, and made a quiet wish, so far under his own breath that scarcely an alley-rat could hear him.

It was on his way back into the building when a low rumbling sound bounced off the maze of inner-city walls and into his ears. The reverberations crept closer and closer until the first of three bikers rounded into the alley, off Milwaukee Avenue. Every window in the building shook as if in dread. Ashes from the tip of his cigarette vibrated off and crashed through the escape's steel grate to the alley below. To avoid revealing his perch on the fire escape's corner he extinguished the remaining portion of his smoke and took shelter in the shadows.

The Bikers appeared burly and formidable. They were dressed in black leather and followed by a pink, SUV limousine. Al crouched in the darkness to observe them travel directly below his position and park. Then, to his disbelief, he recognized one of the bikers.

With all his wealth, Al's brother hired a live-in housekeeper from Mexico. She helped him do things around the house that his lazy ass wouldn't do, but Al had never seen her so nearly undressed. Before he took a breath, the limo door sprang open and out popped two loud guys in blue pinstriped jerseys followed by a blonde female biker. When the cycles shut off, the gang leader approached a pair of large steel doors attached to the adjacent building. A passing Blue Line train drowned out the voices, but it eventually passed by, allowing Al to hear them. He listened attentively to the voice and was shocked that it was not a man at all – it was a woman!

Al thought he was hearing things or perhaps the Biker had a higher pitched voice, but he was not mistaken, it *was* a gang of Biker women. The Capitan called for silence among the gang, and then, the baseball fans started laughing and punching each other. The Blonde smacked them in the back of their heads and whispered to them to, "Shut the fuck up, I mean it, or *else.*"

One of them giggled loud enough for Al to hear him whisper back to her, "You promise that?" So, she smacked that one in the back of the head, again. Then the other screamed, "Oh yea, well I got more guts, lots and lots more *guts*! More guts than that pussy!" After he was done, she slapped him repeatedly until she became bored of smacking him around. Furiously, she reached down the back of his pants, grabbed his underwear, and pulled until he lifted off the ground. When he started to whine, she stripped off his belt and gagged him with it to avoid any further disruptions.

The Captain collected herself and again demanded silence. She stood directly in front of the steel doors and spoke. Just before another Blue Line passed by, Al was certain he heard her utter the words, "*Release It*!" At that precise moment, the massive steel doors swung wide open. The Capitan entered last, allowing her guests, then the other bikers to pass before her into the building. After the Capitan entered the building, the steel doors closed behind them all.

The Tale of Big Al

Beholden by his natural curiosity, he watched for his brother's housekeeper and the Bikers to depart their hideout. He waited in the shadows long enough for angst to drive him to reach for a smoke, but before he could spark one up, the steel doors groaned open. Bubba's housekeeper, and a brunette biker emerged as the doors shut behind them. When they mounted the Brunette's ride, it backfired with a thunder from summer condensation inside the motor. The reverberations shook Al's footing on the rusty escape as they drove away down the alley. Their sound melted away into the city, but his curiosity at such odd activities summoned his patience to wait, so wait he did.

He waited and waited, had another cigarette, then waited some more before becoming tired of waiting. After nearly an hour had past, Al felt drowsy so he laid down again on the escape to stare at a few stars not bleached by city lights. He wondered what Bubba's housekeeper was doing with Biker chicks. As he gazed at Orion's belt, Mintaka star, he became sleepy and slowly slipped into a sublime subconscious stream of waves that drew him into a dream. He lunged onto a giant pile of down pillows and sunk into the fluffy mass. Faster and faster, he slid through the down on a spiraling pale blue ribbon, like a spark upon lightning.

Al fell into an opening – a seam or crack in time and space – and wound up in a place much like where he was from, only smaller or larger depending on perspective. In this place, he was not an average six-footer that he was in the old world. Now, he was a giant able to step over trees as he would have stepped over weeds in the old world. Rivers did not reach big Al's knees and scarcely a lake came up to his waist. Sure enough, big Al, was a giant in this strange new world!

As hours led to days, days led to weeks pride overcame his common sense, and big Al vainly cried out, "WOW! Is there anyone greater than me in this new world?!"

Strange as this new world was to big Al he heard a voice speak to him, *"Be humble, big Al. I have many servants in this new world who are much greater than you."*

Determined to find someone greater than himself, despite the strange voice, big Al walked the breadth and width of the entire new world. All big Al could find were average sized men, who generally ran from the lurching giant to avoid being crushed. All seemed lost for big Al, until a short time later.

One day, after a long day of looking for someone greater than himself, big Al became tired and looked for a place to lie down. He came across some strange rolling hills that resembled human feet. He propped himself up against one of the hills and watched the sun slowly melt into yellow, purple, then red before dipping away into the horizon. It was not long before big Al fell asleep. In the new world, like the old, it became chilly at night so he awoke in search of better shelter from the cold. Not far away, only a couple steps for a giant, he found a large cave where he sought sanctuary for the night. Once inside, he felt his way up the interior of that cave which was rather warm and comforting considering the cold outside. Big Al nestled up against a couple warm boulders, and fell back to sleep, very soundly... until early morning.

Unexpectedly, there came a rumble, which roused him from his slumber! There was a violent commotion all about him then all at once, he flew out of the cave and landed on the ground! Big Al got up, frightfully rubbed his eyes, and wondered what beast he disturbed inside the cave. Suddenly, the hill, cave, and general landscape moved and stood up before him raising a small dust storm that blinded him for a few moments.

After most of the dust settled, Al saw it was not a hill or cave at all. For behold, it was an extremely *huge* giant, sure enough, much bigger than big Al!

As bellowing dust slowly settled about him, he shouted and screamed at the giant, but failed to get his attention. The giant was so tall, only a faint peep reached his ears. Finally, he took notice of him and picked him up. He placed him into the palm of his hand, like a bug or other insect, for examination.

"Who are you and where did you come from?" demanded big Al, with his hands on his hips; a dusty coating of powdery earth blanketed his body.

Naturally, perplexed by such a question, the giant replied, "I'm a lost shepherd boy. I have an older brother greater than me and we live with my mom and dad. One day my brother and I disobeyed our father and he became very angry. So angry that he put us in his sling and slung us far, far away and in opposite directions, to separate my brother and me thoroughly…. Who are you anyway, and how do I get home?"

…And from that time on, Al, took pride in being humble and never boasted of his greatness, again. Then, the giant dropped Al from his palm and as he fell, he kicked him in the head.

"Wake up! Wake up, you lazy, good-for-nothing, bitch!" his brother screamed. He shoved his feet off the escape's railing, causing it to shake and shuttered. "What the fuck are you doing asleep on the job, jackass? Is this what I pay you to do for me?"

"Shh, somethings going on, what time is it?" Al asked, rubbing his head from the initial kick. "It's 2:30 you fuckhead! I've been waiting for you downstairs in the bar, like a fool. You're damn right somethings going on now, you lazy…" Al interrupted, "No, no, you don't understand."

"Oh no, I understand plenty. Just look at yourself, you lazy piece of …"

Then, before Bubba finished his curse, the steel doors creaked open. Bubba stopped and looked around, not knowing what made the loud noise. Al grabbed him, and pulled him into the shadows. Once he pulled him close enough, he whispered in his ear, "*That* is what I was trying to tell you, do you see now? Shh, let's listen and watch."

This time, Bubba did as Al instructed and huddled close. Both watched the Bikers emerge from the structure. The Capitan led the gang, who filed out one by one, past her. Once all the Bikers past her, and she appeared satisfied, she turned toward the steel doors and clearly spoke, "*Grab It!*" and, the steel doors shut. As each of the Bikers straddled their respective cycles, Al noticed that the men, the ones wearing blue pinstripes, were not with them. Careful to conform to the exact pairing order, they rode back out the same way they came, following the Captain out of the den.

The brothers tracked them by sound for about a half-mile, to Division Street, when the thundering motors faded away into the stillness of the city night. Bubba quickly stood up, intending to descend to the alley and investigate. Al did not descend instead, he insisted on diligence.

"We should wait patiently for the Bikers may return if they forgot something, or for some other reason. It's reasonably foreseeable before the fact, they'd discover us, and such an encounter will likely include very bad consequences for us", he explained to Bubba.

Despite his restrained admonitions, Bubba insisted they, "… get our fucking ass down there now, when the city is quiet and before they come back. We'll hear their motors a half-mile away and hide. Stop being a wuss, you fucking pussy!"

After some brotherly backbiting, Bubba's persuasive argument won the day. Ultimately, it was the curious gambler inside both that burned with desire to know what they did not. Since Al could easily recall the words the Captain used to open and close the steel doors, his curiosity dictated tactical conduct to execute Bubba's big idea.

They hiked down the fire escape's rusty stairs to the alley below. They nearly lost their footing during the decent on two occasions. First, a rusted rail gave way when chunks of loose iron broke away from it. The second happened when a brick popped from the building at an anchor point on the wall. The brick and other debris fell to the dark alley below, echoing off walls upon hitting the ground. As they lowered from the final corroded rungs, they quietly listened for any sound of motorcycles.

When none approached, they stood in front of the steel doors and noticed something odd about them. Instead of a doorknob, it had a huge brass and copper lock set directly in the middle of the double doors. The lock was at least a foot square, which was not what made the lock especially strange. The locks' unique design had no keyhole, and no dial for a combination.

Alternately, it had a woman and a man cast in an amber shade of copper. The woman's portion of the lock was standing above the man, gripping his penis with both hands. The man was naked lying flat beneath the woman. They thought this was bizarre enough to examine, so they crept closer, crouching in the darkness to get a better look. Then, Al whispered the words he heard the Capitan speak ... *"Release it"*... but nothing happened.

"What did you say?" Bubba asked. "That's what she said when...",

"No, she didn't say whatever you just mumbled. I heard her clearly say, '*grab it*'", Bubba interrupted, though he had no idea what he was doing. He never saw the Bikers enter the abode and had no knowledge of those words, but Al did.

Al thought this was peculiar for he was certain she said those words to open the doors to begin with. He decided to get a bit closer; leaving Bubba crouched in the shadows. Fearlessly, he stood before the steel doors and clearly said,

"Release It".   Suddenly, the lock sprung. The copper cast woman **SNAPPED** and released the man's penis, then, just as they had done before, the doors slowly creaked open.

***

EXPLORING THE CITY CAVE

The brothers did not dilly-dally outside long, they entered immediately, and the doors shut behind them when they did. Al knew the secret way to open them so he wasn't concerned about being locked inside. Though he brought a flashlight, he did not need it.   They quickly realized this wasn't some dump, another inner-city warehouse, this was a very special place.

The first thing they saw was an interior awash in pale moonlight, illuminated through a massive skylight four floors above. A milky-shade of light poured itself into the building, like sparkling water, gently spilling into a still pond. An ornate seating area surrounded by bookshelves lay in the center beneath the moonlight. The interior spread out from the middle, beyond the well-lit center where they saw a huge, vaulted warehouse, heaped with goods. The old department store that now hid a posh palace of goods was cavernous in its height and depth.

They walked in slowly…at first, then broke into separate directions. Al walked to the left, drawn by collections of fine leather furniture and thick, velvet sofas, chairs, and chaises. Bubba went to the right where there were hand-carved dining tables and place settings for twelve, arranged like a formal dining room. Hanging over the table from rafters forty feet above was a massive chandelier at least four feet in diameter.

Made of crystal, it hung from a link chain anchored near a buffet table and china cabinet.

Al ventured farther inside behind the furniture area where he found a few fine cars, a silver ghost, an antique limousine, and a few others that he didn't even know. Lined along the back brick wall was a fine collection of very select motorcycles. There were crates stacked high and deep throughout the abode. Piles and bales of coats, designer dresses, suits, fine bolts of silk and brocade filled vaulted side-rooms. Magnificent carpets numbering in the thousands from Tabriz and Isfahan lined the floors. Rolled like tree logs in a lumberyard, the carpets were stacked along one entire wall. Closer to the dining area Al saw a section of bookcases arranged with rare old beer steins, bottles and ar'gillehs (a middle-eastern water pipe, made of glass or metal and attached to a hose; commonly known as a hookah).

On his way to investigate a menagerie of chests on the adjacent side of the building, Bubba saw something twinkle in the moon's opaque light. Two neatly stacked rows of luggage and bags, piled five feet high, made a meandering path for some thirty feet back to the dining area. As he walked past a French-made leather duffle bag, he noticed something sparkle inside, so he reached into it. It felt cold and heavy so he pulled it from the bag.

"What the ... no fucking way," Bubba whispered to himself, when he held the ingot of pure gold in his hand. He discovered a dozen gold ingots carefully arranged inside the bag. He looked inside three or four bags of fine luggage that created the path. Depending on the size of the bag, each one had at least a dozen ingots. He estimated the number of bags lining the path to be in the hundreds, perhaps thousands. At that moment, he realized this was a very special hiding place, a secret preserved not for years, but for generations of thieves!

"Bubba! Hey Bubba, where are you?" Before responding, he held a gold bar in his hand, its heavy weight pulled at his greedy pride, like gravity upon a wayward space-rock.

"What the fuck, Bubba… where are you?"

"Over here, take a look at what I've found over here."

Al came down the path and randomly, Bubba unzipped a bag. He reached into the mouth of the bag as if unnaturally plucking a child from a womb. When he pulled his right hand from the bag, he held a glistening gold ingot shamelessly above his head.

"Feast your eyes, Brother!" he shouted boldly, before he began to slowly tip to the right from its weight. Al's jaw dropped, bedazzled by the gold, before he said, "Holy Shit! I'd think you stole this, this fucking bar of gold, if I didn't know better!"

"Bull shit!" he retorted. "I'm no thief, unless I'm so considered for stealing this from Biker thieves." He held the heavy ingot in his right hand

and declared, "I know where to find as much wealth as we can imagine."

Al, who was the darker of the two, turned a pale shade of white and sat down on some of the bags. "There, right there you're sitting on a million dollars in gold, or more. Amazing isn't it? But even then, there's just so much more than that, it's beyond our *wildest dreams*!"

"Well Bubba, I do have some *wild dreams*, but this, this is just…"

"Oh, I know you have dreams, brother. Trust me, I know, but this place is beyond that."

"Yes, yes, but this place is even beyond your own greedy little mind where your would-be aristocratic dwells, Bubba. This is crazy! What are we going to do with all of it? Even if they are thieves, they'll find it missing. Why should we steal from thieves, anyway, why do as they have to acquire wealth?"

Bubba frowned at his questions and was about to answer when a bottle on a nearby bookcase jangled then rattled against another. The brothers stared at each other then heard the low rumbling sound of motorcycles approaching. Their eyes bulged as both nearly screamed but panic quickly turned to action as they tore for the exit. The sound grew louder and louder as they ran back along the path. By the time the brothers ran through the moon lit center they heard them coming north on Milwaukee, from Division street. They sprinted through the middle and into the dark opposite side to find the doors, their exit.

Just as Al was about to utter the words to open them, Bubba said, "No, wait I'll be right back." Then, before Al could stop him, he bolted back to the opposite side, his footsteps echoing away. He reached into a French-made leather bag and pulled out a bar with his right hand and another with his left. Al patiently waited and when he saw him dashing back into the moonlight, he uttered the words, and the doors sprung wide-open. They rushed out, but when they exited, no sooner had the doors shut than the cycles approached the alley's entrance.

He handed one bar to Al who cradled it close to his chest, like a football. "Follow me, brother, to the back door. I have the keys, come on." They ran to the back of Bubba's neighboring building and opened the lock. Bubba lowered his shoulder and gave the service door a good shove to get inside the building. Bubba left the door partially open so they could hear their motors growling. They heard them idling near the six-points, until they rode northwest on Milwaukee and away from them. Once their sound faded, they felt safe inside the building to talk about what they discovered inside the hideout. Stunned by the amount of wealth in gold and possessions, the brothers immediately began plotting a way to go back and explore more. However, Al was not as convinced as Bubba that they should steal from thieves.

"What bullshit! They are criminals, gangsters on motorcycles. They won't report crimes to the police, what would they tell them, 'Hi, we're bikers and we want to report the theft of our stolen goods.' No, of course not, that would be ridiculous!" Bubba chided before concluding, "We should go back in there, right now! We take as much as we can, as quick as we can and split the take fifty-fifty, keep it simple."

Al was convinced that, "Stealing anything from anyone is always risky. Stealing from criminals, such as bikers, is ludicrous, Bubba. They'll find us, they won't need to go to the police, they need only go next door. Then, maybe they'll stop by and say, 'Hello Mr. Qizil, we are the criminals who stash our cash next door, here. We know you lifted our goods, now be a good man and please give'm back?' Naturally, they'll kill us. We should be patient. Diligently, observe them and learn their patterns very, very carefully. Then, construct a plan that is certain to work. Why risk anything less for the greed goading us to chance such unforgiveable mistakes?"

Bubba would not budge to take stock of his brother's reasoning, rather, he insisted they go back in, the sooner the better. After debating to near argument, they realized it was three in the morning. They agreed to meet up later that day at Bubba's club and observe any patterns of biker behavior, then determine whether to execute a plan. They agreed this would be a one time job, one and done, sharing everything fifty-fifty, then went their separate ways home.

Al wrapped the ingot in a dirty rag from the back room then hustled down the alley. He ran to Milwaukee Avenue, past some sewer rats that scuttled away behind a row of over-stuffed city garbage bins before walking to his van. He put the bar in the passenger seat next to him and drove a short distance home to Logan Square in his van. Once inside his house he removed it from the towel and rubbed his hand across its smooth surface, admiring how it glistened in the faintest light. Though he wanted to examine it, he was too tired so he tucked the bar under his bed and fell asleep.

Bubba drove home too with other plans in mind. He immediately contemplated going back before sunrise that night sans his brother. His pride dictated conduct to satiate his greed, the goal. "Why should I share it with him?" he thought regarding his brother, as he prepared his SUV to carry bags of gold out of the Biker's cache.

•••

CUT OR UNCUT?

Joe watched the Junky jump after the lights in the dark distance, hazy night sky above. When he saw the lights drift down an alley, he decided it best to leave quickly, without drawing attention. Joe walked little more than a block from the park when out of the darkness popped the same girls he stopped earlier on the sidewalk. They smiled widely when the Redhead, wearing a shameless grin, politely asked, "Pardon us, Sir. May we ask you some questions?"

Joe smiled back, his deep dimples agleam and said, "Sure, is this about the park?"

"As a matter of fact it is" said the Purplehead.

"Did you see any green lights, here at the park?" asked the Redhead.

As the interrogation continued on the sidewalk, Joe revealed that he in fact, "saw many different colored lights, not just green. I think the other guy saw them too. He was chasing them. I think he caught a green one, then I accidently scared him and…"

"We know, we were watching you from over there by the dog run. We wanted to see if you could really see them. Did you see the garbage can tip over?" the Purplehead asked. "I did, the lights did it, they were hiding in the can, and then they tipped it over from inside the can, I think. The other guy chased after them."

"Yea, uh… we didn't see that. We thought only the other guy could see them. Do you know the other guy?" the Redhead asked him.

"No, I just saw the lights, he seemed to see what I saw so I…"

"So, you can really see them, like that other guy?" the Purplehead asked him.

"Well, yes. That's why I stopped you to begin with. I saw all these lights, but you really can't see them?"

"No silly," the Redhead replied as she gently brushed up against him with her shoulder. "You're different; most people can't see them, it's rare, you can. That's what makes you different … and very sexy because of it."

The girls, who were now more flirtatious with Joe, explained that those 'lights' were, in fact, the 'jinn or genies' of Wicker Park.

"Yea baby, haven't you heard?" asked the coy Redhead.

"Heard about what?" he replied.

"Ha, ha … all the gin … get it? You know, all the evil spirits around here, silly boy." she said, as her braid jabbed and tickled Joe's nose. Again, she gently rubbed up against him, and asked, "Does this make you excited?"

Joe stepped back a bit and asked, "What should I be excited about? That I've seen these jinn or *evil spirits?*"

"Well, well, look at Prince Joey. Hey, he's a cute when he gets scared, huh?" the Purplehead blurted.

"Yea, he is!" replied the Redhead. She curled a long braid in her finger as she smiled at Joe.

"Oh, I know he is," echoed the Purplehead, as she circled him, like a piece of meat, eyeing him from top to bottom, very carefully.

"Ok, ladies… Look," Joe was getting a little anxious. Despite being a bachelor and strong, he was by himself and he wasn't sure what these girls wanted from him.

"I own the pastry shop around the corner from the Six-Points ... I don't know what I saw but I *do* know ..."

"Shut up, silly boy" the Redhead interjected seductively. "Are you a member of the Tribe?"

Joe thought she meant baseball, so he replied, "No. No, I'm a Southside fan though I live on the north side." Joe smiled, not to be rude, in case she was a North-sider fan. Then, the Purplehead giggled, "Hee, hee, wrong answer, silly...."

"Well, you *are* a silly boy, aren't you? What we mean to say is ... are you Jewish?" the Redhead explained.

"Jewish? Am I, Jewish?" Joe was not expecting an inquisition about his sincerely held beliefs, so he refuted, "What sort of question is that? What exactly *do* my religious preferences have to do with the park, huh? Is this code language for some … uhh."

"Of course we're not bigots, silly boy. In fact, I'm half-Jewish myself."

"You *are?* I didn't even know that and I've known you for how many years?" the Purplehead asked.

"Not now, just let him answer the question." They waited for what seemed a terminal period before the Purplehead asked, "Why don't you just tell us if it's not such a big deal? Why make a big deal about it, right? Alternately, why *is* the question such a big deal for you to answer? Why don't you just answer the question, mystery man?"

"Well, if you must know …" he said. Joe was confident he met the cut, despite not being Jewish, so he answered the question.

"No…. No, I am not Jewish, but I still may be able assist you anyway, if you're really interested in those sorts of personal specifics."

Joe was a youthful and healthy looking forty-five year old. Before he became a successful pastry chef, Joe was something of a ladies' man in his youth. Since beginning his pastry shop, he worked too often to maintain a serious relationship with anyone. Joe was about to ask them if they wanted to hang out later that night, when a car screamed passed them on Damen Avenue, its horn bellowing. As the horn faded, the Purplehead asked, "Hey…. Are you Middle Eastern?"

"Middle Eastern, huh? No, I'm an American. I think I know what you ladies are looking for and I don't think I'll disappoint," replied Joe confidently, a scoundrels' smile pasted on his scruffy face.

"My, my you are a sexy boy, tonight, aren't you?" the Redhead said.

"Will you just answer the fucking question, already? What's the big deal, are you an Arab or not?" the Purplehead demanded.

"Wow! First, my religion was an issue, now my *ethnicity* is an issue. Look, is this about the orbs flying around in the park or something else?"

"I'm so sorry, Sir. My friend and I are just excited right now. We are excited to meet you since you may have seen something in the park tonight, and well, your ethnicity may have something to do with it, objectively".

Joe was a firm believer in free enterprise as much as freedom of expression. He did not want to disrupt the girls any further with his immutable characteristics, let alone risk the reputation of his local pastry business. So he decided to serve the girls what they wanted, "Well, if your question really – and mean *really* – has something to do with the things at the park tonight, then … yes. Yes, I am ethnically … Semitic, uh, an Arab Semite."

"Great, that's great." said the Redhead, "Wow! A natural cut diamond," she giggled devilishly. He wasn't sure what she meant by diamond, he assumed she was talking about the same thing he was, so he acknowledged, "I'm not sure I'd call it a diamond, but yes, I am cut. I am circumcised to perfection."

Raised according to his family's Islamic traditions that required circumcision, baby Joey had no choice. Since no Imam was available to perform the ceremony, his parents thought nothing of taking him to a rabbi for circumcision. However, for the girls' purposes he was 'cut' in other ways. Poor Joe had no inkling that to them, his circumcision was not the only way he was 'cut'. Unlike most diamonds that are in the rough and catch a little light, few others are naturally 'cut' to capture light. To them, his eyes had many facets that saw deeper into reality than most others could. This made him 'cut' in many ways, and to the girls, he represented an opportunity, like winning the lottery.

After he declared his ethnicity, and the girls stopped laughing, they invited him to an after-hours party later that night. They exchanged cell phone numbers and agreed to meet at Club Luca later that night. The Redhead wanted to, "chill over cocktails and chat before the party."

Joe was ecstatic, so after a friendly good bye, he hustled the rest of the way home. He ran upstairs, and as soon as he got into his apartment, the cool central air hit his sweat, giving him a chill. He went to the bath and ran a steamy hot shower. He drew the curtain around the inside of the tub, and then let the shower water trickled down his back, tickling his memory.

As a young man, Joe loved booze, babes, and occasionally, some late night bacon on a cheeseburger, too. He kept most of his indiscretions secret from his family, until he got married. Before becoming a pastry chef, Joe traveled for business as an insurance adjuster. He was on the road for days, sometimes weeks, at a time without seeing his wife.

Once, when a large flood hit the middle Mississippi valley, Joe traveled to the Memphis area for a job adjusting insurance claims. One night after a long day of adjusting many claims, he went to his hotel bar to decompress with a cocktail. While there, he met the bartender, an archetypical southern belle. She spent the night in his hotel room, that night. Days later, after he returned to Chicago, she showed up at his home while his wife was shopping. When his wife returned, she caught them in a steamy shower together! For a while, things got a little tough for Joe but he persevered and bounced back. Now, years later, he was going to hook-up with a couple hot ladies for some late night fun just like he used to, or so he thought.

•••

EMPTY BOTTLES OF JINN

After the girls said good-bye to Joey, they headed to the six-points to meet a very special friend. For the girls, late night cocktails and friends were more ordinary than a roll in the hay, but he was special. They knew that Joe, the well-cut baker, would come to them later that night.

When the girls arrived at Stella's Lounge, they immediately went to their special friend, the Biker Captain. After they embraced, the girls sat next to her in the corner booth and explained their tardiness. Normally, being late was not something that needed explanation, but in this case, the girls felt so compelled.

The Redhead explained that they were walking down Damen when, "all of a sudden this Joey looking guy, shows up and,"

"But his name *is* Joe, right?" the Purplehead clarified.

"Right, his name is Joe, he's the baker over here around the corner," the Redhead replied, "but didn't you think he was kind'a all, like *Joey?*"

"Oh yea, yea he was *so* Joey!"

"Right? It's like, 'you go boy, pound that strawberry pastry!'"

After the girls exchanged high-fives, the Captain said, "Wait, what the fuck, what do you mean, all *'Joey',* what the fuck is that?"

"Oh," laughed the Redhead, "it means he's built with big, broad manly shoulders, making him sexy, and then he's actually *from* Chicago."

"Now, that's a cherry on top, right … mine!" the Purplehead laughed. Their swag prompted them to jump on top of the table and start dancing. Erotic jostling would understate their perverse choreography. After they finished, they sat next to each other and sipped on their odd mélanges.

"Are you two done, now?" asked the Captain. "So, I get it. Joey is some hot fucking man, right?" The two nodded their approval, still supping cocktails. "But what does he have to do with Chicago?"

"The expression, 'Joey' is like, 'Uncle Sam',"
explained the Purplehead.

"How so?"

"Well, the City is like all, *Joey,* as the United
States is like, Uncle Sam."

"Right, right.   For example, Boss … the
Aldermanic system is all, *'Joey',* because it's so
corrupt," the Redhead explained, as the two girls
agreed, nodding at their Captain.

"Ok when you two are done talking about
our friends down at the Ward Offices, maybe
your giggle group can get back to what the fuck
happened at the Park tonight, huh?" The Captain's
frustration at her underlings' adolescent behavior
motivated the Redhead to explain, "Alright, so *Joe*
stops us in front of the park.   He points to
someone jumping around by the fountain, and
asks if we can see him.   We say, 'yes', then he asks
if we can see … get this, 'glowing balls of light
that the other guy is chasing'. "

The Captain's interest grew as she continued her story:

So *then*, he tells us that he can see the lights and is shocked that we can't. He didn't appear drunk or fucked up in any way. He just said he could see what the other guy saw. He even tried to point them out to us, but you know, we're not 'cut' that way. We did take a closer look to validate his claim and what we observed was very interesting. We know he's telling the truth, he saw the same thing Ralph did.

"*Ralph!*" she screamed, "He was there? What the *fuck* was he doing there?"

"*Oh, yes* and this guy, Joe the baker, saw the same thing Ralph saw because they talked about it, they talked about the jinn in the park."

The Captain, who had been smiling, now frowned and became quite serious.

"Wait, wait, and slow down here. You saw Ralph and this guy, Joe, talking together, *too?*"

"*Yes!*"

"And this guy, Joe, was so fucking cut that he could see the jinn in their natural aura ... and then, he talked about that with Ralph, too?"

"Oh yea, and not only was Ralph there talking all about this issue of ours, but he was trying to catch them, again, too."

"Fuck, this is un-fucking-believable. I go out for a cocktail thinking I'll unzip stress, then all this crap blows up - *great!* How about we have a shot now, and then ..."

BUZZ, BUZZ, BUZZ

The Redhead's cherry red phone vibrated between various empty bottles and cocktails spread over the table. It caught the attention of all seated in the booth, so she checked the text. "Ok, he's on the way, we better split," she said, before hailing a Uryder from her phone.

The Captain insisted they bring him to the soirée and then, "once you've got him there do him real fucking good upstairs. This may work out perfectly to our advantage. What we've wanted all along will be ours in the end." The girls understood her instruction very well and embraced her before getting into their waiting ride to Club Luca.

Proud and cool, she straddled her cycle parked outside but on the inside, she felt different. She knew only one person who saw jinn, and that was not Joey. At one time, she felt something like love for him, but now she was brimming with jealous hatred for Ralph.

The Junky, properly named, Ralph, had contact with her partly because of his gifted ability to observe jinn and partly to feed his own addiction. After capturing them in his brass jar, he'd deliver them to her. In exchange, she gave him an unknown quantity of heroin, thought to be pounds. This swap for services rendered between them continued for some time, whenever Ralph was lucky enough to capture one.

After a capture, he'd diligently follow a specific procedure to transfer the light, like a firefly, from his brass jar to its own antique bottle. Once released into its unique home, he'd seal the bottle with an insignia that the Captain gave to him. The emblem was exclusive to each bottle and acted as an ancient signature that sealed the jinn's fate in the bottle, until released by a new master.

The Captain and her gang acquired the collection of ninety-nine bottles by inheritance from mentors in crime. The original gangsters allegedly obtained the bottles from the vault of an antiquities shop in Baton Rouge they robbed many decades earlier. However, others claimed the artifacts were stolen from a cave, far, far away, in the Yabrud region of the Middle East centuries ago. In either case, it was well before the Captain's tenure that the original thieves acquired the mystical collection of ancient carafes.

Glass and silver were the bottles primary components. Each was individually idiosyncratic in size, shape, and color. However, the glass of each was opaque, purportedly kilned from Middle Eastern sand and capped with a unique seal crafted from silver. For those with knowledge of such dark arts, the intrinsic value in these objects was incalculable. The singular problem was all the vessels were empty, making Ralph a valuable partner to the Captain and her gang.

Ralph captured five jinn, which he turned over to the Captain. Seduced by such power derived by gift, she began to imagine bearing a child with such an amazing ability. However, just as she let her guard down two jinn mysteriously escaped from their respective urns. Ralph promptly caught them a couple days later in exchange for more heroin. The Captain thought the coincidence so peculiar that she had him followed, she wondered, "what the fuck is he doing with so much white dragon?"

Later, she proved to be a craftier criminal than he was when she caught him cheating on his end of the bargain. It is unclear how exactly he did it, but somehow he used the jinn he captured to release the ones he'd caught earlier. When she confronted him with this double-cross, he declared, "I'll do it again!" to feed his glutinous addiction. Freedom for Ralph hinged on satiating his addiction to heroin, his real master, subsequently denying him any choice at all to quit. She would have killed him then because he served his addiction before anything else. However, his ability to benefit her required control of her vengeful nature, thus, she spared his life. Instead she had Ralph brought before her, where she violently humiliated him in front of the gang as merciful punishment for theft. Trust, which is scarce among thieves anyway, eroded to naught when the Captains' desire for revenge ripened into a reality for Ralph. Joey now seemed the perfect candidate, a perfect fit for her master plan to breed cut children.

When Joe stepped out of the shower and briskly dried off, he heard his phone chime for text. He doused his body liberally with fragrant

American cologne then walked into his bedroom to check his text. The Redhead's message read:

"Ur BFNs can hardly wait 2 c U! Don't b late or u'll miss the best part of the night ... afterhours! Ciao, Joey!"

Club Luca was far away from his apartment so to get there by eleven he broke into a full body sweat enroute. By the time he arrived, he removed his blazer but sweat rings hung from his armpits and down his back. He looked at his phone and saw it was 10:59. It was crowded inside, so he stayed by the entrance to dry off. He quickly saw the girls, but before he could approach them, two bulky blokes abruptly bump into the Redhead causing her to spill her cocktail onto the Purplehead. Since it appeared they might know the two men, Joe thought it best to wait and watch from a corner near the entrance.

The men were markedly drunk, wobbling and leaning too much to be sober. It was difficult to tell if they knew each other as the Redhead put her arm around one, and then they embraced.

The Purplehead just sat at the bar calmly sipping her cocktail, not caring if her fishnet leggings were wet with whiskey. Then, the Redhead wrote something on a napkin and handed it to one of the men. Both men analyzed the note carefully before leaving the napkin on the bar. The girls giggled at them as they did, before they bid them farewell with hugs. They hurriedly threw back their cocktails forgetting the note on the bar, altogether. They meandered around the bar, before the Drunkards wearing baseball jerseys, finally exited the club. Then, when the girls were alone, Joe strolled over to begin his lively plans for the night.

•••

PLEASE, HAVE A SEAT

Intoxicated with pride and gluttonously filed with booze, the Drunkards followed the

Blonde out of her exulted cabal. They passed through a horde of partiers, wet with sweat, back to the entrance before she led them outside to a pink SUV limo.

"Can you believe how fucking rude some people are? I'm mean, dude, she didn't have to throw our drinks at us if we ... whoa, now that's what I call a hot rod and driver!" said the Artist, as the driver stepped out in a pair of black thigh high boots. She had short, slicked-back hair that matched her black leather jacket over white bikini bottoms.

"Holy shit, would ya' look at that, she's gon'a open the door for us, too. Sweet!" the Musician avowed.

"That's right boys, you enjoy the ride. Pour a cocktail or two, get comfortable and I'll be right back." With her party plans thoroughly interrupted by the drunken duo, the Blonde's tarnished pride dictated irate revenge. The driver closed the door after they were inside and the Blonde gathered a small group of her underlings to stage a small party in advance of their arrival. The Captain led them out of the foundry compound and to their stash on Milwaukee Avenue. On the way, the Drunkards debated between samples of each alcoholic beverage available in the limo.

"No, dude I saw her first when she asked me if the bar was dead," the Artist refuted after sampling some anisette.

"We'll see about that, I think the Blonde chick wants a piece of me solo, Bro. Why don't you talk to the leader, you know the older chick with the eye-patch?" suggested the Musician.

"*Me*, and that bag of haggis, are you fucking kidding?!"

"She's still hot. She's hotter than anything you've had recently besides your right hand, *man*."

"Right, I just can't see me with that old eye-patch chick, aw'right. Uh, I don't know maybe if it was pink *and* heart shaped too, I'd consider her, but seriously she's scary don't you think?"

Their collective ego bordered on the edge of a narcissistic utopia. They joked, not at all aware of the fate that awaited them when they arrived too quickly to the sanctuary. "*This* is as far as we're going, babe? Can't we cruise around a little more, perhaps with you on my lap, naked? Come on, I got nuts and I got guts. Wha'da ya say ya let me hit a homerun in the back yard, baby?" the Musician grabbed his testicles during his comment.

The Blonde was not amused at all, so after a brief delay in the alley outside the abode to straighten her playful guests out, the Captain uttered the magic words, and they entered the sanctuary. When she released the belt from around the Artists mouth, he untucked his underwear while whining. They socialized very little inside the inner sanctum before being hustled downstairs to a room covered in white ceramic tile from floor to ceiling. In the middle of the room was a five-foot high, black chair. The four legged iron chair was peculiar and bolted into the floor. It had leather straps on the armrests, and legs. Most particular was the eight-inch diameter hole cut into the middle of the seat.

"Ok, who's first?" asked the Blonde slowly circling the chair before she rounded the duo. The Captain and a few specially invited guests meandered into the room to enjoy the show. The Artist volunteered, "Sure, I'd love to be your muse", he joked, but not for long. He presumed she was a high-end dominatrix and he was sitting in her dungeon's iron chair. She stripped him naked then strapped him into the chair, good 'n tight. She climbed up behind the chair on rungs that attached to its stilt-like legs. When she got to the top, she reached around to the front and firmly squeezed his nipples, causing them to bruise and bleed slightly. When he squealed, she slapped him, and then it started to get sadistic.

"Fuck yea! I've wanted to do that to him all night!" hollered the Musician, blowing smoke out his mouth. He shook so much from nervous excitement the ashes from the tip of his cigarette fell into his cocktail. He may have joked easy, but his hosts did not.

After she gagged him, she crawled under the chair then pulled his limp dick and balls through the hole. She gently caressed and stroked his cock with one hand and licked her middle finger on the other. As she stroked him harder and harder, she slowly inserted her moist middle finger up his ass, then two fingers, then three, then four ... then she shoved her entire fist! She slowly burrowed her hand deep into him, tunneling up her arm to her elbow. She quickly pumped her fist up inside him four or five times, his screaming muffled by the gag. Then, on the final thrust, she extended her long, sharp nails inside him, ripping a giant hole in his rectum. What happened next was not screaming, but what happens to a human voice when malformed by sadistic torture.

Even some of the harden Bikers left the room at that time, rather than hear such horror, but not the Musician. He still shook now, not from demented excitement, but from the realization that he was next. She dumped the Artist's body on to the tile floor, with a thud, as blood sprayed from his anus. Chunks of intestine dangled from her bloody hand when she turned to the pale Musician, shaking in dread, and spoke "You said you had guts, you said you had nuts, you told us all about it didn't you? Well let's see what kind of nuts and guts you *REALLY* have and let me hit a homerun in *your* backyard. Please, have a seat."

After extracting their revenge, they left the bodies on the tile floor to bleed out what life they had left. The Captain then led her gang out of the Biker's city cave, down the alley, and hastily back to their soirée.

Only a few blocks away Bubba calmly sipped a large cup of coffee in his back yard patio. He gazed at the stars above without an inkling of fear for his selfish greed lulled his common sense to sleep. He wore his lucky black Southside fan hoody, careful to dress in all black just in case he needed to hide in the dark. He was ready to move the Biker's fine jewelry, gems, and gold. He tossed five large duffle bags on top of a couple old wooden trunks. In the backseat, he loaded several suitcases and travel bags. He intended to fill each with as much treasure as he could greedily pack into them. Driven by fanatical pride, he denied any risk of stealing from Bikers to satisfy his greed. However, in his zeal, he overlooked one critical detail and such ignorance would cost him.

From the safety of his SUV, Bubba followed the shadowy, narrow alley running parallel to Milwaukee Avenue that led to the Biker's lair. His headlamps flooded the alley corridor with light. He saw the two giant double doors and he backed the SUV's rear-end up against them to park. Before exiting his ride, he saw nothing but a couple large alley rats, fat from scrounging in the refuse of the posh local restaurants. He slowly approached the building, keeping close to the

SUV. He crept near the door and quietly uttered the words he heard the Capitan speak… "Grab it", but nothing happened. Bubba thought it was strange since he was certain those were the magic words he heard the Captain say. He decided to get a bit closer, thinking perhaps he wasn't loud enough to be heard. Again, he crouched down in the shadows and spoke, "Grab it!" yet again, nothing happened. Surprised by such an unexpected circumstance, he started to sweat profusely and worse, he needed to pee from drinking so much coffee. Suddenly he recalled that Al said something else, something he could not remember. He never paid attention to what Al said to open, not shut the doors.

At that moment, he realized he'd made an ignorant mistake and needed to abort his mission. "Fuck! I should've stuck to the plan," he wistfully whispered before he heard the echoing rev of motorcycles approaching!

Locked in his steps, he remained silent and thought to leave immediately but before he could, they turned down the alley, coming quickly, coming closer. He scrambled for a place to hide when he saw parts of the alley illuminate. As his intestines dropped from fear, he found a spot to conceal himself between a couple steel dumpsters. He wedged his butt between the bins and stayed there in the crouched position as the Bikers funneled in behind their den.

The first thing they noticed was an SUV parked behind the building that didn't belong to any of them. They carefully surrounded it, circling as if it were prey. Suspicious at the circumstances, the Captain ordered her troops to quickly, fan out through the alley to secure a perimeter and watch for any strange movements or noises.

"Any sugar over there?" Bubba heard one biker ask another, passing by his hidey-hole. She stopped only feet from him, scanning diligently about as her biker boot-heels rapped a rhythmic step. She even struck the bin next to him with her knife to see if the trespasser would spook, but nothing happened. She diligently hit the following bin as he squatted in shadows, motivated by absolute fear to stay in place.

Crouched in the same position just wouldn't work for him, he needed to pee so badly he felt like he would burst. After another five minutes past, he felt his prostate would pass through his urethra if he didn't go, so he let loose a river. His hope was no one would notice or confuse his pee for garbage juice leaking from the bins. He watched the urine saturated his inner thighs and leached a stream between the bins, slowly pooling near an alley drain cover.

"What the fuck is that?"

"That's nothing but fucking trash sauce", the other Biker responded. The Biker who noticed the seepage, walked toward the source, in front of the bins. She saw the trail go between the bins into a dark blind spot. That's when Bubba made his move using his dagger to lunge and stab the snooping Biker in her shoulder. They both fell in the alley, rolling into his puddle of piss, before they got up and slipped on the wet alley. Flat on his stomach, he got up, surrounded by Biker-chicks. He tried to bolt through them, like a running back through a defensive line, but after colliding into one, a couple others managed to stab him as he ran past. Bubba fell again, but this time they caught him and wrestled him over on to his back. They lifted his hoody, and flayed him open in the alley with an eight-inch Bowie knife, his guts poured out of a thick slice to his belly. In a desperate attempt to snatch back his life, he tried to put his intestines back into his lower section, but another Biker knelt behind him and slit his neck half way off.

Still gushing blood, they quickly dragged the writhing body into their compound. A red stained trail followed them inside where the Captain delighted in what they caught. She ordered them to, "Toss that loser into the pile of other loser shit, we'll get rid of them later, after they bleed out." Her troops loyally threw Bubba's lifeless body onto the floor still oozing blood.

"What the fuck happen to them, cheering for the wrong team again?" one Biker asked the other, who replied, "Probably, who the fuck knows, maybe the Boss hates baseball. Let's get the fuck out of here."

There, Bubba's blood seeped through his black Southside hoody creating another stream that gathered, like swollen water behind a levy. Bloody Northside jerseys draped over the pair of Drunkards, now dead.   Together, their blood comingled into a red pool on the basement floor.

•••

WELCOME TO NYMPHOTICA

Joe leaned against the bar and said, "Well, hello there, ladies. I've been…"

"You showed up! *Awesome-sauce*!" screamed the Redhead, hugging and kissing him. "Oh yes, *so* nice of you to join us," said the Purplehead, kissing him overtly on the lips then licking the bottom of his earlobe.

"Well, thank you ladies so much for such a warm welcome. I must apologize for being late but I didn't wish to interrupt your conversation with those gentlemen and…".

"*What*! Those drunk dorks were not gentlemen at all, they were just a couple fuckos", the Purplehead explained. "Really, we don't know them at all, they came up to us. We had to get rid of them, they were really drunk and getting too touchy, you know?" the Redhead added.

"That's only part true, I saw them run into you. Then you", he said pointing to the Redhead, "spilled your drink on her. Now, isn't that how it happened?"

"My, my, but you have been waiting patiently for us, haven't you? How thoughtfully humble you are Joey."

"Yes, well ladies, I think we may want some cocktails before we, uh, start it up this evening." Before the Redhead replied, she looked at her partner and said, "Can you believe this guy, he's so..."

"He sure is a sexy slender man and very ... uh, what is it, *um... courteous,*" the Purplehead disclosed, before she nibbled on his neck then bit it so hard that, "*OUCH!*" she made him scream.

"So sorry, you're that good enough to eat, Joey boy", she explained, as the Redhead pinch his nipples. "*Hey!* Uh, I can see you ladies are definitely interested in fun, so why don't we finish our cocktails and split this scene?" he proposed, trying to be hip.

"Oh my, and he's so touchy in those sensitive spots, huh? Okay, we'll play your way to start, but ..." the Redhead paused to caress his crotch before finishing, "this cock is ours later, agreed?"

"Of course, let's toast on it," he gregariously raised his glass toward the girls, interlocking their liquid salutations for carnal receptions later. After that round, they had such a good time they opted to have one more, then the ménage et trois reveled on the small dance floor.

"Ooo lala Joey, where did you ever learn to move like that," the Purplehead whispered in his ear, then, bit it, grabbing his firm ass at the same time.

"Well," he whispered back, "if you like that now, you'll love the other special endowments I possess, later." A small crowd gathered, to witness them savor the splendor of the moment, embracing, intertwining their bodies and lips. It was not long after that, they were on their way to party so the Purplehead used the Uryder app on her fancy phone to call for a quick ride.

"Is that a friend of yours?" asked Joe. "Who, *Uryder*, you don't know what Uryder *is?* They're your best friend when you've been drinking, or it's just a fun way of getting around sans a car or motorcycle."

Three minutes later, a black Uryder SUV pulled up curbside and they rolled to the party in extra-large luxury. On their way, they passed over the Cortland Bridge when Joe glanced out the window and saw the same two men in Northside baseball jerseys who ran into the girls at the bar. They were yelling at the Junky he'd seen earlier at Wicker Park, but he didn't say anything about it as he was too busy being fondled by les femmes fatale to care.

While driving through the maze of warehouses and buildings to the party, they flirted with Joe, kissing and caressing him. Then, the Redhead grabbed Joe around his button down collar and said, "Okay, seriously you have to remember this. We can't fuck around at the door so you have to get it right. Listen closely, to get in you have to say, '*I'm here to have a wild night, a good morning, and a spectacular afternoon*', you got it, Joey?"

"Of course, I can do that, *ahh*, no problem", he replied, as the Purplehead nibbled his neck and sucked on his earlobe.

"Oh really, what is it?"

"Uh, I want a good night and great morning … uh."

"*Right*, it's hard to remember isn't it? Okay, remember it's … *hey*, can you please *stop*, we need to be serious now," she said, so the Purplehead stopped sucking on his neck and stroking his thick dick. "Okay, you have to remember to say, '*I'm here to have a wild night, a good morning, and a spectacular afternoon*', you got it, *now*, Joey?" she asked before she licked his lips.

"*You have arrived at your final destination*," the Uryder's navigator chimed. When they pulled up in front of the building Joe saw all the motorcycles and a gigantic pink SUV limo parked on the side of the house and thought, "hmm, this is a little strange ... even weird, but so cool!" Joe the baker was so elated to be invited that he'd done anything the girls said to do.

"Hello there, I'm here to have a wild night, a good morning, and a spectacular afternoon ... was that right?" After Joey repeated the secret phrase to pass, the threesome indulged in shots, coke, and high-end cocktails from the bar. They laughed, flirted, and teased each other as they drank more and had fun ... *until* they encountered the Drunkards a short time later. Before the Blonde escorted the unwanted guests to their urban cave, she instructed some underlings that hastily lead the trio away down a tiny passage hidden behind a liquor closet. They climbed a narrow spiral staircase to an opulent sanctuary upstairs above the party.

"Bienvenue, and welcome to Nymphotica! This is our private boudoir, Joey!" the Redhead said, extending her arms outward.

"Holy shit! Is this your place?"

"Is this place mine? Oh no, this belongs to my friend, our boss, silly. She's not here right now, though. We're the only ones here, Joey, so..." With her innuendo clear, she unfastened her bustier, exposing her perky size Cs. They made the most of such opportunity, quickly disrobing and rolling onto the bed.

Alabaster marble covered the walls and four sandstone columns supported a domed skylight above the bed in the center of the room. Surrounding the bed was natural candle light, muted by flashing lightning in the sky from approaching thunderstorms. The bolts burst light that reflected wildly off a giant mirror, hanging above the bed. Crackling thunder vibrated the glass skylight as they engaged upon an arena of cool silk sheets, in a bare embrace. Their swollen drops of body sweat spattered the linen when the chamber door opened. Through the doorway's opaque light slinked the Purplehead's slender silhouette, gripping a magnum bottle of

Champaign. Her bare bronze skin exposed by the crackling atmospheric charges that sparked in the night.

"I thought my friend could join us ... I didn't think you'd mind?"

"*Mind?* Why on earth might I mind? Of course, I thought we were in this together, come on in and join the party, babe!" he responded.

Then the three made their way to an adjoining room. It had crisp white marble walls and floors save for three black interlocking circles embedded in the floor. In the center of the circles, surrounded by five burning candles, was a ready-made bubble bath. The oversized tub illuminated by red lights under the water could have fit five or six adults quite comfortably.

Lustfully, the girls passed their stud back and forth, like a pair of gluttonous sisters, devouring a bucket of buttery popcorn at a movie theater. Their bare bodies pressed and rubbed against each other in the steamy water when the

Redhead noticed something poking through the bellowing clouds of steam. She whispered into Joe's ear, "Well, since you don't seem to be a satisfied customer, *yet*, let's check you out again, mister."

"Babydoll, I can go more, I'm built like a thoroughbred for a reason", when his wet body exited the tub she slapped him across the ass and said, "Good boy, *smack* that's what I want to hear."

"Now that's properly motivating me!"

"Oh yea, get in there and lay down", the Purplehead demanded, pointing toward the bed in the opposite room. They tapped into a sexual fisher inside him, and sculpted his lust, compelling him to feed his sexual ego, his manhood, his pride.

Joe had the stamina of a horse, besides other endowments, but he was getting tired. He asked for a little bump, "... you know, uhh, some nose candy?" By dating himself, so frequently with pop vernacular from the eighties, the girls knew he must have been the stud back in *his* day. Ravenously, they all dosed up their noses before they entwined themselves into a lathery, loaded orgy of sexual bliss, *again*. This place was a narcotic independent any drug induced pleasure that Joe ever imbibed.

When Joe and girls finished treating themselves to debauched pleasures of the flesh, the group enjoyed a good smoke. They adjourned to a salon that adjoined the bedroom. They drew from a large crystal globe-shaped hookah as they laid on humongous pillows scattered about the floor. After each had their draw, the Redhead suggested enjoying the magnum with iced oysters before the Purplehead proposed one final fit of fun.

"We'll tie you up then, fuck you again, except this time we'll inject you with some special bump sauce. Trust me, Joey, it'll take you where you want to go."

It looked like an oversized red velvet chaise. It had leather straps on the arms and legs. Perhaps, in a past life, it was a high-end therapists' cushy couch for clients. Joey laid back and became very comfortable very quickly, feeling the soft velvet pet his bare backside. The Redhead tied him down with the straps then mounted him like Lady Godiva. As she did, the Purplehead pierced his left arm with a needle, "Ouch," he quietly whispered. Then, she crawled to the other side and pierced his right arm with another needle. In one, she injected a heavy dose of heroin, while in other she slowly drained him of blood. The blood spurted into a giant glass beaker, before she shut off the valve. She didn't want him to bleed out before she had her last turn to ride their well-cut man. She took her jaunt when the Redhead finished, quickly hopping on top to milk his leftovers as the Redhead slowly opened the blood valve to finish draining him of life.

His blood pumped and sprayed into a canister until it slowed to a trickle, tinting the glass red. Joe felt a little dizzy and lightheaded but kept driving hard until unloading deep inside his final vessel. Before he knew it, he slowly … very slowly … passed out into a deep and satisfying slumber. Joe's six foot three, body lay on the chaise limp and lifeless.

"Fuuuuck…. Look at him there, like a hibernating bear or something" said the Purplehead. "Yea, well he's done his job; it's time we do ours. *He* doesn't matter now, but what we carry inside us does," responded the Redhead before she kissed her partner, gently caressing her lower abdomen.

Unfortunately, for Joe his unsuspecting good nature left him vulnerable and victimized by the treacherous nature of the girls. He slept without dreaming, nothing but blackness strangled his thoughts, until one by one, he could not remember anything either. It plucked pieces of his life and threw them away into an abyss, forever lost in the bottomless black. The next thing Joe felt was floating, swinging back and forth until jostled nearly awake. He felt a dry, overwhelming thirst, and heard voices but could not understand them. He saw bright lights flashing in the darkness, but nothing else. He wasn't sure if he was dead or alive, but he felt lighter than air, so he thought, "maybe this is how I'm supposed to feel after a night like this one".

He felt so light, that he floated away into the universe atop a cool, dry breeze, like a surfer on the crest of a perpetual wave. He felt the air gently embrace his face one last time before Joe, the baker, drifted away from this reality and into the spirit world, forever.

•••

<u>SERENDIPITY</u>

Sunlight bathed the intersection's Coyote building, centerpiece of Wicker Park, when Al arrived at his brother's tap later that morning. He crept around the corner to the back alley and found nothing but trash, rats and a couple alley cats fighting over a discarded piece of chicken. He thought Bubba must be at home still asleep, so he backed out of the alley and drove to his house. He pulled into the carport expecting to see his brother's SUV in the garage but it was completely empty. Al waited, thinking he went to the store to buy doughnuts or coffee. After a while, a jet-black European sedan slowly rolled up curbside and stopped in front of the home. The rear-door opened and Emjay sluggishly lazed up to the side doorway, under the carport. His jaw dropped when he saw her up close in a pair of black thigh-high boots, a mini-plaid skirt and, a black leather vest. The vest was too small, as her moonlighting gig required such attire though no one, beside Bubba, knew it. She worked as a stripper off Division Street at, 'The X Lounge', a place the Bikers roosted often enough to encounter her.

"Well, good morning," Al greeted her before asking, "Uh, have you seen Bubba?"

"Aye, que huevon! He should be up by now."

"Yea, I know what you mean, but his SUV isn't here. I'm doing a job for him on Milwaukee and he was supposed meet me at the Tap this morning."

"That sounds like him, he's probably asleep. He makes too many plans and then can't finish them. He'll probably show up in few minutes, late of course, like usual. Let's go inside, come on." She pushed the sticky side door open with her shoulder. She looked for Bubba, calling out his name several times, but her calls rang hollow.

Emjay amended her birth name, 'Maria Juanita', after she arrived from Ciudad Juarez, Mexico. Obviously, her reasons for the change related to the social stigma of smoking wild weeds. Though she enjoyed, 'la mota en la noche', she definitely did not wish to be confused for a drug trafficker, so she felt very comfortable changing it.

"I would offer you coffee but, I'm going to bed, it was *too* long a night for me," she explained.

"Yea, he'll probably roll into the car port any time now with coffee. *Hey,* before you fly off to dreamland, I was going to ask you, did you go out last night?"

"I went to a party, a very late night party. I just got back, like *now,* so I'm ... ahhh," she yawned.

"I can see that, so I won't keep you up, but I really think you may want to know. I was working late last night too", he went on to tell her about how he saw Bikers go into the building next to the Tap. Then, as he told her, "Uhh, Al," she said, "d–did you say these bikers were, *chicks*– women, girls on motorcycles?"

"Yes, that's correct… it's a gang of Biker chicks."

Emjay paused to shiver from sleep deprivation, an aftershock of the moment, and then stuttered, "This sounds strange, but I think I know who you are talking about. If you saw them last night at that building you must have also seen…"

"*You*, yes I saw *you* ride in with one of them, a brunette Biker, but then you left before everyone else."

"Please excuse me, I'm still a bit shaken…you don't understand what I saw," she said.

"No, no, please, just have a seat here. Take your time", Al said as they sat on the foyer divan to talk.

Emjay went on to explain that after two years of moonlighting at The X, a definitively large group of bikers started to visit the club. They'd visit the club every night for a week or so, get very rowdy, drunk, and stay until very late.

Then they'd disappear and not return for another few weeks.

"What's so bizarre about bikers behaving like that? That's what *they do*, isn't it?" wisecracked Al. She shook her head explaining, "They are criminals, traveling from town to town, city-to-city, robbing people. For sure, they meet in Wicker Park to store newly acquired goods in their special hideout, the building next to the Tap. I made a terrible mistake tonight and went with them and ... well they're weird, violent, and very dangerous. We should be so wise to stay entirely away from them."

Al's jaw dropped again, as did his bowels when she described everything he'd seen including herself being there. He realized she knew as much or more than he did about them so he encouraged her, "Please, go on. You left with the Brunette before the other bikers, *why?*" he asked.

Ok...she invited me to a private party, ok? I had a little trouble tonight at the club and she helped me out. I left work early and went with her to this freaked out party. Anyway, it was awesome-sauce, but I had a problem down stairs in the old foundry basement. She called it, 'the show' and made it sound more like a fancy home theater or live entertainment. It was very hot and smelled like sulfur, a thousand burning matches. I was sweating and had a metallic taste in my mouth, just like el Chuco. In the cellar, they have a giant blast furnace where they smelt heavy metals, like the smelter back home. So, they were booking bets at the time. I had no idea what sort of propositions, until a couple, big alley cats were put into a penned area, like a big chicken coop, so they couldn't get out. Then, they unleashed, all these rats into the pen, like dozens of jumping and leaping rats. The rats started gnawing, biting, and scratching at the cats. The cats fought back … it was loud, people at the party screaming for the cats or the rats but it didn't matter. In the end, the rats ate the cats, and those pigs all cheered for more. That's when I knew I had to leave. Then we went over to their, '*secret hideout*', and that's when things got so fucked up I had to leave there *too.* So then, we rode back to...

"*Of course!* He drove his urban tank back there. That fucking double-crosser, double-crossed *me!*"

"Huh, who are you talking about?" she asked. "It's my brother, besides lazy, he's the most greedy, dumb-fuck I've ever known!"

With great haste, Al drove his van to the Bikers' abode, leaving Emjay to sleep. He parked his van in the alley, away from the Biker's secret entrance in case he needed to flee quickly. When he got to the entrance, he was surprised to see a trail of blood, drying and covered with flies along the ground. The trail led to the double-doors where it ended. He shooed away the flies and stood before the doors to enunciate the magic words.

When they opened, he saw his brother's red SUV parked just inside the doors. He slowly peaked inside, around the vehicle and saw the sickening sight, naked bodies suspended from the ceiling. His brother's body dangled over the SUV dripping with blood, to send a twisted message to anyone who might claim the body. Two other swollen bodies hung from the rafters nearby. He recognized the pair of baseball fans who went inside the night before, but never came out. It was so gruesome he immediately began to mourn his brother despite the danger to his personal safety for spending too much time in the den. He wrapped his brother's body in some fine linen he found among the treasures and carried him on his shoulders to the doors. Golden sunbeams blazed between buildings and down the gangway when the doors groaned opened.

Al loaded him into the back of his van, placing his body under a painting tarp. Then, he diligently drove away, fearing Biker lookouts. Nervous sweat stains rung his collar, chest, and armpits as he wiped the beads from his brow, and drove to Bubba's home in Humboldt Park. Luckily, just as he drove away on North Avenue, the full gang of forty Bikers roared into their hide out from Milwaukee Avenue, serendipitously missing Al.

The Bikers immediately noticed the missing body and began accusing each other of conspiring to steal from the group, arguing to the point of shoving. The Captain spoke up first and loudest over the chattering group of bikers:

Who among us would dare betray our gang by stealing from a sister? This obscure threat has come from outside, not inside, sisters. As we can all gather, the body of, a *man*, is missing here, but the other limp dicks remain undisturbed. The thieving cohorts were only interested in taking the Southside fan, not our other friends dangling here. Well why on Earth did they only take *him*, was he the next best thing to a World Series Trophy, of course not sisters! These are crafty fucking gangsters who think they are trifling with us but they are bloated, bloated with vanity! They know how to enter, yet have the self-control to resist the temptations of our treasure.

Whispers among her thirty-nine underlings broke through the silence as her sisters sought comfort for their worries about the cache's security, so she continued:

Now sisters we know the presumptive thief we caught was aware of our sacred place, luck that we happened upon him before he could enter. Someone other than this missing motherfucker knows how to get in and whoever the fuck *that* is had the motive to be so specific about which dead motherfucker to take. Proving more than one thief has discovered our den. Our decades of hiding fortunes in plain site are over. If we are not diligent, we will slowly lose all the wealth we've amassed with great toil for all these generations.   We must start by keeping guard here every second of every fucking day, beginning now. Tomorrow is one day closer to finding the conceited motherfuckers who thought they could steal from us. We may even find them by tomorrow, but until then we hunt for them immediately.   Since we don't know how many know the secret words besides the missing fucker and his gang, we must hunt down and kill all who may know. I'm angry and I demand revenge, what do you say, bitches?! *Do you agree?!*"

They approved the Capitan's scheme with raucous applause, shouting and whistling. In fact, the group got proactive and unanimously agreed to cease any further criminal activities and devote their collective energy to the single task of pay back.   So impressed with her crew's dedicated devotion, she said, "I expected nothing less than exactly such *testicular fortitude* from my gang of bitches but this… this vengeful spirit is what will deliver the heads, legs, and arms of the remaining thieves to us even faster."

The forty Bikers were like a hungry beast hunting for a meal to satiate their lust for revenge, until gluttonously extracted from its prey. Now, Al's more or less humble life was on a collision course with the Captain and her biker gang from hell.

•••

© 2016 pending

www.ingramcontent.com/pod-product-compliance
Lightning Source LLC
Chambersburg PA
CBHW060620130626
46555CB00002B/584